Cursed Wolf 2

Iron Beast Pack

Angelica Aquiles

CURSED WOLF

Developmental Editing: Heather Fox at Fox Proof Editing

Editing: Heather Fox at Fox Proof Editing

Cover Design: Francesca Michelon at Merry-Book-Round

Formatting by: Angelica Aquiles

Contents

Dedication

To all the badass moms out there holding it down! You guys are all amazing!

Triggers

This book contains adult content and mature language. It is intended for readers 18+.

Please note this is Reverse Harem which means Kat will not choose between her lovers.

Possible triggers include blood play.

Enjoy!

Chapter One

Tyler

"Tyler help!"

Kat's terrified scream echoes in the hall all around me, more panicked than I've ever heard her. My computer bounces off the floor with a thud as I take off back down the stairs at a breakneck pace.

As my feet hit the bottom step, a jolt of electricity pulses through my veins like a sudden burst of fire, nearly taking me to the floor as I skid into a crouched position next to Kat.

Benji is on the ground convulsing, his teeth smashed together in a pained grimace. As his body relaxes all over, Kat's face drains of color, and her lips part in a gasp. "Is he dead?" she cries.

"He's alive, but I don't know how much more of this he can take." I dig my fingers into the side of his neck, feeling his erratic pulse.

"What's happening to him? Did Dan's pack do this?" Benji is squirming from another wave of pain, and Kat's eyes begin overflowing with tears at the sight. I can't imagine how my brother is handling this. Another pain rocks through me and my body grows cold and sweaty. It's getting harder to breathe, but I know that Benji is shielding us from the worst of the pain. I want to tell him to let go, to let us handle more of that burden, but if I open my mouth now, I may not be able to hold back my screams a moment longer.

Loud footsteps are coming from outside, and I know who it is before she even opens the door. As if she can sense something is wrong, Amara swings the door wide, worry lacing her face. She stares down at Benji with round eyes and then drags her heavy gaze to me.

Kat's eyes glow and change colors as she takes in the pretty redhead, violence mirroring in the depth of those beautiful violet orbs. She watches Amara's every move, tilting her head in her direction. I wonder if she knows she no longer looks human.

The panic lighting Amara's face gives Kat the wrong idea about us, and I can practically feel the tension as a low growl bubbles up her throat. When this is all over, and I can finally explain things to Kat,

I'm sure the girls will get along great. They've both had many challenges in their lives, and both have been betrayed by people they loved.

My pain intensifies, and I hiss, doubling over. Kat instinctively reaches to catch me, but Amara jumps between us and grabs Kat by her wrist. "Don't touch him." Kat looks shocked and narrows her eyes as two more witches stride in, each pulling a gurney. I try to move toward Kat as her eyes slowly focus on Amara's hand that is still clamped around her arm.

"Take your hands off me." Kat's voice is slow and methodical, and Amara is smart enough to do as she's told.

"It's nothing personal, I promise. My guys will move him, okay? They have more experience with this."

I see the hesitation and fear in her face as she watches two perfect strangers get down on the ground to tend to Benji. Her eyes are so full of love when she watches him, and I wonder if she watches me the same way. I wonder if I take up space in her heart too. It's scary how quickly she's become the center of our world, and I care so deeply for her that it's killing me to not be able to stand and take her in my arms.

The two men gently grab Benji and move him to one of the gurneys while he's still thrashing around. We've always been able to share each other's thoughts and pain as bonded Alphas, but Benji is trying to shield us from the worst of it.

"Amara, tell me this isn't what I think it is?" My Alpha voice holds so much power, and though I normally don't use that tone, it's just how my body responds when no other Alphas are present. Benji and I like to approach things in a friendly manner, so we normally let Ash take the lead.

"I'm not sure yet. I have my theories but want to confirm before I say anything." I glance over at Kat again, who looks like her whole world has been crushed. I want to hug her, reassure her that my brother will be fine, even if I don't know for sure, but I can barely move.

"I know you know, Amara. Cut the shit and just tell us. Is it the curse?" Kat's sharp gaze turns to mine. "Is it finally time to collect?" My voice booms through the entrance, creating an echo throughout the house. Kat looks at me with her mouth wide open in shock. I'm in too much pain to care that my Alpha tone may have scared her, now isn't the time for apologies.

She looks at each of us vacantly, schooling her features. Her eyes hold so much sorrow. Not only did the witch we've been hunting fuck us over for over a hundred years, but she fucked over Amara's family too.

My phone rings. I'm still crouching down next to where my brother was a moment ago, but it's too hard for me to reach into my pocket. Thankfully, I don't have to say a word because Kat grabs my phone for me, answering it and leaving it on the floor with the speaker on. She watches me carefully like she doesn't want to hurt me, but she has so many questions she wants to ask. She's biting her lip hard.

"What the fuck is going on, Tyler? What the fuck is this pain?" Ash's voice pierces through the speaker, but it's almost like he's in the house with us by how harsh his tone is.

I close my eyes and rub them before answering. "I'm not sure. Benji collapsed, and Amara is here trying to help him."

"Is it the curse?" I look up at Kat to see her reaction, but she's schooling her face the way Amara did earlier. I can't get an actual read on her, or maybe I could if I had the energy to really look.

"The witch is close, I can almost feel her in the air," Az says from the background.

My heart rate quickens at the thought of finally catching the witch we've been hunting so long. We almost had her a couple of days ago, the same witch that did this to us. The one who hurt not only us but all the witches as well.

Amara's sister.

Chapter Two

Kat

There's a soft hum, and on a normal day, it would drive me nuts until I found the source, but instead, I'm staring at the two guys I've fallen deeply for. One is on a gurney, borderline unconscious and withering in pain, while the other looks like he's two breaths away from falling on the floor.

Then there's this pretty girl Amara who keeps touching Benji, and my wolf and I don't like it one bit. If she wasn't trying to help him, I'd have thrown her ass out the moment she jumped between me and Tyler.

Over the past couple of days, this place has been more of a home than any other place I've lived.

With Theo, I never felt this welcome or wanted. I just didn't realize how toxic that whole relationship was until I left.

Even if two of the men who occupy this household don't want me, I still feel like this is where I belong. I can't explain it. It just feels right, as if my whole life has led me to this exact place for a reason.

I watch them leave with Benji as two other guys help Tyler toward the second stretcher. My heart is heavy watching both of them in pain, not knowing what I can do to help. I'm feeling kind of useless, and I hate it. I want to take care of them the same way that I care for my kids when they're not feeling well. Maybe it's the mom in me, but if someone's hurting, I feel the need to help.

When my men leave, it's only Amara and I standing six feet apart from one another. She doesn't stand in a threatening position, but she keeps her eyes on me, taking in all my features. I do the same to her as my wolf and I assess her weaknesses. My wolf is wary because she got too close to Benji and Tyler. It's so strange that I never used to look at people this way, but now it comes sort of naturally without meaning to, definitely the animal in me.

She breaks the silence with a genuine smile. "It's nice to finally meet you, Kat. I've heard so many good things about you." Instead of saying something to sound civilized, there's a defensive rumble coming from deep in my stomach. "I'm not trying to hurt you." She takes a small step toward me and I tense up. She's either really brave or really stupid. My wolf is in control right now, and she's not afraid to pounce and kill if she needs to. The thought of murder should scare me, but it's become a matter of fact. "I promise." She holds her hands up briefly, surrendering, showing me that I have nothing to worry about. "I'm actually the one that told them to go get you."

She takes another step forward, and I contemplate whether or not to get ready and attack, but so far, she hasn't given me a reason. Benji and Tyler didn't look like they disliked her, so I stand still, at least for now.

She takes another step toward me putting us at touching distance. She watches me with fascination in her gray eyes. There is something familiar about them, but I don't think I've ever met her before. The hair on the back of my neck immediately stands. "I'm sorry," she puts her hands in the air. "I didn't mean to spook you, honestly. I'm a friend." Her voice is warm and filled with hope. She's taking a chance right now and she's hoping it pays off.

I stare at her for a moment longer before asking, "What's going on?" I look to the door where my guys left, wondering if they're going to be okay. After I finally find two people that I care deeply for, they nearly die.

She sighs, tirelessly crossing her arms and looking at the floor for a second before looking back up. "They were cursed over one hundred years ago." My eyes widen slightly. That's what I figured, but they weren't forthcoming with that information, though I'm not sure why.

"Would you come out and say to someone you've just met that you're cursed?" My wolf asks.

I think about it for a moment. *"I guess you're right, I wouldn't tell people, that seems too... personal."* Although I think I've gotten pretty *personal* with Benji and Tyler.

Amara mumbles something, but I don't quite catch it since I was having a conversation with myself. She clears her throat and speaks louder this time. "We need to figure it out and fast."

"Why now? Why has the curse been activated after so many years?" What does this moment in time have to do with anything?

"I'm not sure why it hasn't been activated until now." She's hiding something more about this curse. Her heart keeps jumping a beat. She's nervous.

"Who put the curse on them?" She holds herself tighter for comfort, and I almost feel bad for her. I don't know her well enough to put my arms around her or reassure her of anything. I'm not wired that way. I have to be wary of new people since I don't exactly have the best track record of trusting the right ones. Trust came so naturally with Benji and Tyler, it's like they're an extension of myself, but I can't say the same for the girl in front of me with nervous eyes.

She sighs deeply like she's carrying a huge burden, and now I wish that I was able to give her that hug she needs. "My sister." Her voice is so small, but I hear her loud and clear.

As the words come out, a tear runs down her face. She wipes it away, clearing her throat. "She uh...she killed thousands of witches to obtain the power that she has now. She's dangerous and unstoppable." Shit, a strong witch that can't be stopped sounds bad. "So many witches died and so many families suffered." She hangs her head low. "She put a curse on the four of them."

I stop her this time because I must ask, "Why did she curse them?"

She looks back up at me. "Because they're powerful." She hesitates for a moment before saying, "They had their own unique magic." My eyes widen.

Well, it looks like my men just got more interesting.

Chapter Three

Ash

"Drive faster, Jackson," Az growls from the back seat, ready to rip the poor wolf's head off.

"He's doing eighty in a forty-five," I spit through gritted teeth. I turn to the back seat to face my brother, who is sweating bullets with a white-knuckle grip on the door handle beside him. He's falling apart, just like me, but he wants blood as payment for our suffering. I can see the familiar gleam of revenge in his dark blue eyes.

"I should have stayed." Az is a control freak in every way and unpredictable to onlookers, but I've known him the longest, and I know exactly what would have happened if we'd stayed. "We were so fucking close," he seethes, leaning his head against the cool window and squeezing his eyes shut.

"You know how manipulative and smart Amara's sister is, if you had stayed behind in this much pain, she woulda got the jump on you. She's too fucking clever to catch on a good day, all it takes is one mistake, one missed moment while you're doubled over in agony, and she'll be so far gone. Who knows when our next chance will come." He doesn't answer me, but he knows I'm right.

"What if this pain isn't tied to your curse?" Jackson's nervous eyes hit the rearview mirror when he asks the question that's been on all our minds.

"The last time I checked, your job was to drive the fucking car, not ask stupid questions. I shoulda left your ass with the other betas to make sure the Silver Dawn Pack doesn't stick around." Jackson gives me a glance in the passenger seat, and I shake my head. If he pushes Az right now, he may not live to regret it. "Even if it isn't the curse, when I finally find that bitch, I'm going to kill her for all the fucking trouble she's caused." Az groans again, sinking further into the seat.

"Only thirty minutes out now, then we can see if Amara has something for the pain until we find her sister," I tell him. Jackson keeps shooting me unsure glances as he speeds through the streets, and his question sits in the front of my mind. We've been cursed for over one hundred years, but this pain just feels different in ways I can't explain. But if this doesn't have anything to do with the curse, why is Amara's sister so close to us now?

We've spent years tracking her all around the world, and when she finally pops up in the same state, the pain hits us like a fucking freight train all at once. This can't be a coincidence, but something doesn't seem right. I have this nagging feeling that we're headed straight for a trap. What else could she want from us?

Unless this has something to do with Katarina...

Amara's ancestors were the ones who warned us about the witch and sent us to retrieve Katarina and her kids. I wonder if this is somehow interconnected.

None of this makes sense. She hasn't been back here since she cursed us, and now she shows up out of nowhere. And if she's here, there is no doubt in my mind that she's coming for us.

Destruction follows her wherever she goes, and if she's planning to make an appearance at our place, we have to get to her first. My brothers and I have an obligation to protect our pack and our people, and she'll have to go through us before she takes any more innocent lives.

Chapter Four

Kat

"What powers do they have?" I ask, curiosity burning through my body. I want to know every detail about the men I live with. It's only fair, they know mine because I'm certain Tyler pulled up all my information when he was researching, and if I know anything about Tyler, I know he's very thorough and doesn't leave anything to chance.

Her shoulders sag with exhaustion. "That's a story for them to tell you." I nod my head in understanding, but it doesn't make that burning desire to know go away. This leaves me with so many unanswered questions. "I probably already told you more than they'd like. They're very private men. You've been weaving your way into their hearts these past couple of days."

I don't know about that. Two of them practically wish I'd drop dead. "So, what do we need to do?" I ask, hoping there is some way that I can help and stop feeling so useless.

"Find the person that put this curse on them. We've got to find my sister," she says with hate-filled words. It's strange to see someone hate their sibling so much. I spent my whole life wishing for a brother or sister to keep me from feeling so alone in this world. Someone that had my back and I had theirs. This is why I love Jess so much. She's the closest thing to a sister I've ever had. We met when we were older, but we clicked right away, almost like we've known each other our whole lives. She understood where I came from and always tried to be there for me, and I've always done the same for her.

"That's why you have to call her," my wolf says. *"You're being a shitty friend right now."* Ugh, as much as I want to deny it, my wolf is probably right.

I can understand why Amara hates her sister, but it's still weird to see how much hate fills her beautiful gray eyes.

My body stills for a moment. There's a soft hum I was ignoring earlier, but it's getting louder. "Are you okay?" Amara asks, drawing her brows together in concern.

I ignore her and walk upstairs. If I was hoping for some privacy, I don't think I'll be getting any. She's right on my heels, probably worried that I've lost my mind.

"You have," my wolf confirms, but she's listening intently to the noise.

"Shut up, wolf," I grumble.

I open the door to my room and immediately go into my drawer. It's not hidden so deep with my belongings, so I pull it right out. I hold up the stick that the woman from the bar had given me, I think her name was Althea. As soon as I make contact, it stops humming. Almost like it was waiting for me to give it my attention. Is this object alive? I almost drop it, getting creeped out a bit by my thoughts.

Amara gasps and I drag my eyes over to her, watching her take a few steps back and putting her hand on her throat. "Kat, where the fuck did you get that?" I hold the useless steel up in the air and wave it around. She dodges like I'm about to attack her with it, keeping her distance as if I'm going to try to kill her with this, but she doesn't know this thing is absolutely useless.

"On my second night at work..." I smile at her, but she doesn't reciprocate, her eyes are sharp, not letting her gaze wander from the object in my hand. "Two ladies came into the bar. They felt old and powerful, and truthfully, kind of scary," I say as I reminisce. It feels so long ago, but it's only been a couple of days. "I'm not sure what they wanted but they gave me this." I hold it up in front of her, and she keeps her eyes locked on it. "I think it's broken, it doesn't do anything," I say as I look inside the hole once again, only staring at a dark void.

"No, Kat," she shouts, and I jump back, scared out of my mind. I'm already on edge and that just pushed me over. "Don't do that." She startles me and I look at her like she's crazy. "That's old, very, very old." She bites her lip contemplating her next words. "May I hold it?" I bring it over to her as she brings both palms up in front of her, completely mesmerized. "Do the guys know about this?" she asks as she inspects the piece of metal carefully, being sure to keep her fingers away from the hole in the center.

"No, I haven't had a chance to tell them. I figured it was something useless, but now I'm starting to think otherwise." Amara acts like it's something dangerous, and I think that I probably should have been more careful with it.

"You have no idea what you have, do you Kat?" she asks, looking at the intricate pattern that adorns it. "Of course you don't." She answers her own question, but more to herself than me.

I stand there for a while, wanting to pace around the room and burn off all this pent-up energy. "So, what is it?" I ask, tired of waiting. She looks up confused for a second like she was entranced, then shakes her head to clear the haze.

"Oh, well what you have here, Kat..." Her eyes sparkle, and I have a feeling I'm not going to like what she's going to say next. "This is the Kiss of Death,"

"The Kiss of Death?" I repeat louder in disbelief that this small piece of steel has it's own name. Okay, not what I was expecting. I snatch it back from her hands and inspect it. "How is this supposed to be a weapon?" Nah, she must be crazy. There's no way this old ancient thing could murder someone.

"Kat, what you're holding can kill any supernatural with one swipe," she scolds. It's now my turn to shiver. Supernaturals are hard to kill. What in the fuck. "It can destroy anything." She looks at it briefly before looking at me again. "Be careful with it. I've only heard stories about it, but if you fall and accidentally stab yourself, you might die." My eyes widen in surprise. Well, now that she's said it, I'm doomed. I can be a little clumsy at times. "Actually, I don't know if it'll harm you since you're the owner, but it can kill the boys in the house, so please be careful with it."

"How is it supposed to harm anyone without a blade of some sort?" I ask, eyeing the metal stick with doubt.

"I'm not sure how it works but keep it with you. You never know when you may need it." She hesitates for a moment. "That might be the only weapon that can kill my sister," she says with sad eyes like it's finally clicked what needs to happen. She clears her throat before continuing. "I'll give you a belt so it'll be easier to carry with you."

"Thank you." I admire her generosity. She doesn't have to do this for me, but she's trying to help me out.

"Kat," her voice becomes somber. "Don't tell anyone besides the guys what you have or people will come after you." I think we might be too late for people coming after me, but I keep my mouth shut letting her finish what she has to say. "That weapon in the wrong hands will be dangerous, and as far as I know, both you and that weapon are the only ones in existence."

"Well, let's hope I can figure out how to use it sooner rather than later. We don't need a trail of innocent bodies on the floor."

Chapter Five

Kat

"I have to check on the guys now," Amara says urgently. She looks at her phone and I look at mine. It's only been a couple of minutes since they were taken away, but she should be with them, not here chatting with me.

"Yeah go. I'll be there soon." Using the shirt laying on my bed, I wrap the cold, metal stick in the fabric for safekeeping before tucking it into my purse.

Once I have the weapon secure, I walk the long hallway toward Ezra's room and knock on his door. "Hey, it's Mom, I'm just checking in."

He immediately opens the door, and I let out a long sigh. The kids have been so quiet through everything, I was starting to wonder if they had slipped out a window or door when we were all so preoccupied earlier.

"Ava hasn't been accounted for yet," my wolf reminds me, and she's right.

"How are Benji and Tyler doing?" His voice is alert, and his eyes wander down the hall like he expects to see them behind me.

I put a hand on my hip tilting my head slightly. "How do you know about that?" I didn't think they'd notice.

Ava opens her door. Ryder, Zay, and Bryson are sitting on the floor behind her, but Cash is missing. I'm about to ask them where he is but she starts talking. "We watched everything from the stairs. We didn't want to interrupt, you looked pretty frazzled and not..." She hesitates as if she's afraid I'm going to lose my shit.

"What is it, Ava?" I'm worried now. What could it be? What made her hesitate? "Ava," I demand.

She bites her thumbnail, sharing a look with Ezra that I can't decipher. They're obviously having a conversation with each other, but I'm completely confused. This is the sibling shit that I wished I had when I was younger. Someone to confide in and be able to talk to this way. I'm glad they have each other, but that's not what I want right now. I want Ava to finish what she was going to say.

"Human," she finally answers, letting out a deep breath. "You didn't look human," she says again, really driving it home that second time.

My heart skips a beat for a moment before saying, "I'd never hurt you guys."

"No, we won't," my wolf agrees.

"Sorry if that spooked you," I say carefully. That's the last thing I want to do.

"It didn't," Ezra replies quickly. As if he wants me to understand that they'll never be afraid of me. "We were trying to give you some space and didn't want to interfere. You were already going through so much."

I sigh walking into Ava's room because honestly, Ezra's room looks like a fucking tornado just hit it, and that's from me standing outside in the hallway. I don't have the energy to tell him to clean his room right now.

I sit on one of her zebra print chairs. Ezra sits on the other side of the TV while Ava settles onto the bed. The three guys remain sitting on the floor, watching me carefully. Maybe I've freaked them out too. "I'm sorry guys. I'm going through a lot right now."

"We know, Mom. This can't be easy," Ava responds looking paler than usual.

"How are you two feeling?" I swallow through the shame and guilt that tells me this is all my fault. "We were basically kidnapped by someone we trusted."

"Hell yeah it was scary." She bites her lip like she's working up the courage to ask me something. "Can I please have a sleepover with my friends?" she blurts out randomly.

I look at the kids sitting in this room. "Not with them." I snort out a laugh as she looks nervously up from her hands. "No, with Tiffany. Cara will be there too," she says with hopeful eyes. She knows that I don't let my kids stay anywhere, not after the evil I saw growing up in foster care. But there's a raw look of anticipation in her eyes. "It'll be tonight. I'll come home Sunday."

I suppose you want to have a sleepover with your friends too?" I ask Ezra watching his mouth quirk up into a smile.

"It'll be at Logan's house." He smiles cheekily, knowing they've got me close to agreeing with them.

"Who's Logan? I haven't met him yet." I sigh, putting my hand up. "Never mind. Let me talk to Ash." I trust his judgment on the kids' parents. He might be a dick to me, but he's got a soft spot for my kids.

They jump up and down in unison. "Thanks, Mom," Ava says.

"I need to talk to Ash," I remind them before they get too excited.

They completely ignore me. Ava pulls out a bag from her closet and Ezra goes into his room. Well, I guess this conversation is over.

I walk out of her room, waving at the boys as I go, and head downstairs to find my men. Following the growls of pain, I find myself standing in the doorway of a room I never knew existed. It looks like a hospital room with ten beds on each side. Five huge windows line the wall, and there's enough medical equipment to fill an urgent care facility.

It smells like alcohol, and I have to rub my nose a few times wanting to sneeze. When you're a shifter, you are so much more sensitive to strong smells. I'm glad I wasn't a wolf when I was pregnant. The smell of boiling water made me want to gag. If I were pregnant now, I'd probably be in my room the whole time, too scared of smelling anything.

Tyler is closest to me. He appears to be sleeping, and I don't want to wake him up. He looks better than before. Color has returned to his face, and he's looking a lot healthier. I let loose a breath I didn't know I was holding onto.

My expectations are high when I walk over to the other bed and gasp, nearly having to hold on to the bed for support. What the hell? Benji looks pale with dark circles underneath his eyes. How is it that Benji looks worse and Tyler looks better? I lift my head up looking around, but there is no one to ask. The growls and moans I heard must have been coming from him, but he's so quiet now.

I bring my hand up to my cheek, coming away wet with tears. My heart aches for him, I can't imagine the pain he's enduring.

Amara walks in from another door that I didn't see at first. It looks to be an office. "Good news, it's not the curse, but the bad news is, I have no idea what the fuck it is." Amara looks up and I follow her eye movements, and my whole body moves when I catch a whiff of sweet vanilla with earthy notes of tobacco.

Ash and Az are standing near one of the windows wearing shorts. It's so weird seeing them without their signature suits. They look less intimidating this way. But how long have they been standing there watching me?

They both turn and glare at me. Nope, never mind, they can be dressed casually and still look terrifying.

"I was able to stop the connection from spreading to you guys. It's definitely magic. I'm having Doc take him to his hospital to monitor him better."

"That's why we don't feel it anymore?" Ash asks. Az remains quiet with his arms crossed and his lips pressed into a tight line. He likes to stay hidden in the background, always ready to attack, but not in this case. His blue eyes look wild as he brings up his tattooed hand and rubs his eyebrow nervously. His gesture looks so out of place for him. She nods her head confirming that what Ash said is true.

"Where is the hospital?" I ask, turning around to face her because I don't dare look back at the two men behind me who look disgusted.

"There's one here. Dr. Carter is expecting both Tyler and Benji. Tyler is looking much better, so this means the source is Benji. What he has is still a mystery." She looks at him again like he's a hard puzzle she's trying to solve.

Her look does nothing to alleviate my anxiety.

Chapter Six

Kat

I've been tossing and turning all night, nerves running through my body. I should have slept a lot more with everything that went down with Dan, but I'm on high alert.

The kids are hanging out with their friends. I asked Ash briefly what he thought of Tiffany's family, and he had nothing but good things to mention. He may not like me too much, but he's definitely different with my kids. I also asked him what he thought of Logan's parents, and he said they're a good family too. Having Ash vouching for the family makes me slightly relieved. I still worry because of my past, though I don't think that nagging feeling will ever go away, but that's probably a good thing when my kids are involved.

I went to visit Benji early this morning, but he was still asleep. He was sweating profusely, and his eyes were red and hollow. Tyler looked so much better, which gives me strong hopes about Benji recovering soon.

I curl up next to my scavenged items from the men in the house. Tyler's hoodie, Ash's tie, Az's pillowcase, and holding tight to Benji's t-shirt. My wolf has been really quiet this morning and hasn't been snarky with me today. Which only means one thing, she's worried about Benji too.

One of the resident doctors, Doctor Carter I believe, has been checking in on him periodically to make sure he's stable. Worry still gnaws on me, but there's nothing I can do. I'm feeling kind of useless and I hate it. I loathe that I can't relieve him of his pain.

I was told they're going to move them from the house to the actual hospital they have here. Amara mentioned the hospital was inside the wards, but she never told me where.

I walk into the kitchen and grab a salad that's already prepared from the fridge before grabbing a fork and sitting down at the bar. I'm eating when the scent in the air changes. There's a low growl coming from my mouth when I hear a giggle.

Az walks in, and right at his heels is another petite woman about my height with dark, shoulder-length hair.

I start stabbing my greens and shoving them in my mouth, not at all angry.

"We can take her," my wolf growls.

"We are doing no such thing," I tell her. This is the second woman he's brought over. He's made his stance clear. He doesn't want me.

"Why is he bringing a woman over at a time like this?" my wolf asks, rising from her post.

He heads to the fridge while the girl sits right next to me. My body stiffens, but I purposely look down at my food and avoid eye contact with them. I hope they leave me alone so I can eat in peace.

I know exactly why he brought her here. "Is there anything you want to eat?" he says, looking inside the fridge. "Shit, hang on," he mumbles as his phone rings. "I have to take this." He gives his guest an apologetic glance before rushing out of the room. When he closes the door behind him, it's just me and the girl...awkward.

She turns her full attention to me. "Hey, I'm Tia," she says in a sweet voice. I turn around to face her.

"I'm Kat." Her grin is contagious, wanting to hate her I find myself giving her a small smile instead. She smells like a wolf. "Are you part of this pack?"

She shakes her head, "No, I'm from a different pack. I'm visiting here for a while."

"Ours, ours, ours," my wolf chants over and over again. I wish she had a mute button because I can't think with her yapping in my head.

"I'm not yapping," she says annoyed.

"You're the newly turned wolf, aren't you?" I flinch at her words. The guys around me say it all the time. It's just having a complete stranger talking about what happened to me that feels kind of personal.

"Yeah," I answer with one word, not knowing what else to say.

"Well, you're pretty popular, everyone wants to meet you. We haven't seen a newly turned shifter in a long time," she says in a chipper voice. There's a hint of worry in her eyes like she knows what's going to happen to me since I was never supposed to be turned.

I shiver at her words. I don't want to be looked at like a circus freak. It was like that on my first day at work, but I ignored it because I was so excited to be making money. I hope the news dies down soon. I don't want to attract any unwanted attention, especially since the council is after me because of something I didn't get to decide for myself.

"Let's go," Az's voice cuts through the kitchen and my stomach roils at the thought of him being with this girl.

She seems nice, but I'm being possessive thinking he belongs to me. *"He does belong to you, to us,"* my wolf chimes in.

There's a ping on my phone and I swipe at the screen to open it.

Unknown: I want the ring he gave you.

I scrunch my eyebrows in confusion. Who the hell is this and why would they want the ring Theo gave me? Now that I think about it, I'm surprised he didn't ask for it, and I completely forgot to give it to him with all the nerves of being free for the first time.

"You should leave it alone and block the number." My wolf is probably right, but I debate whether or not to answer back. Curiosity gets the best of me.

Me: Who is this?

Unknown: It's Krissy.

Chapter Seven

Az

I bring the girl back to my room. I've completely forgotten her name. Come to think of it, I don't think I asked for it when I asked her if she wanted to come home with me. I met her at the Crescent Lounge. She was having some drinks with her friends and that's when I approached her. I almost feel bad about not asking for her name, but I'll make it up to her.

I haven't fucked anyone since Kat moved in with us, and I really need to release some stress. I'm so wound up. The last person I brought home, I couldn't go through with it. I'm hoping this time I'll be able to fuck something that's not my hand.

I'm hoping this wolf will help.

"This girl and the girl from the bar last week are both the same height and have the same length and color hair as Kat," my wolf informs me of the obvious.

"I'm sure it's a coincidence," I reply.

"She's all I think about since she showed up into our life." I keep quiet by not engaging, or else my wolf will ruin the mood.

"Stand right there," I command, pointing next to the bed exactly where I want her. She does as I say, excitement filling her eyes. I know what women say about me. I have weird tastes in the bedroom, I'm too commanding, I like to play with blood, but they all keep coming back. I've found women are afraid to explore their fantasies. Afraid of the judgment. But they don't have to be afraid with me. I test their limits, but I do make sure that's what they want. They give me their control and it's a mutual agreement that benefits both of us.

The only fucking problem with this is that I'm not hard yet. This is the second time in my life this has ever happened. The first time was a couple of days ago. Fuck!

I go into my closet hoping the toys I have will get me going. I grab the red ropes and turn back around, walking toward her. She bites her lip in slight fear, but I can smell her arousal. She wants the fantasy I can provide.

"Take off your shirt." She immediately removes her crop top. She isn't wearing a bra, so as soon as she takes it off, her tits fall out. She doesn't try to cover them or hide. She knows she's attractive and isn't afraid to show her body.

I walk behind her, getting close to her ear, and whisper, "Put your hands behind your back."

She does as I ask. "Don't you want me to take my skirt off first?" she asks.

"I'll tell you when to take it off," I say, not quite my Alpha voice but it's a tone that leaves no confusion of who's in charge.

"Sorry, Sir." Normally those words would have my body vibrating with pleasure, but I don't feel anything, not a goddamn thing. I almost start to worry that my dick is broken, just like every other part of me, but every time I'm close to a certain dark-haired woman who lives here, I have no issue getting hard.

I look down at the woman standing in front me, I have her back against my front. She's the same size as Kat, and I know that I fucking hate Kat more than anything. It's her fault I have a limp dick. I so wish I could fuck this woman in front of me, she's beautiful, but I'm not getting aroused.

"Open your mouth," I demand, and she happily complies. I unzip my pants and pull it out. Her eyes go wide, probably didn't know what she signed up for. My dick is tatted up and I have a piercing.

She has the same reaction most women do. Slight fear crosses her eyes but I'm not letting her go that easily. "Now suck me and make me hard." She watches with hesitation, and I grab the back of her head, fisting her hair and pushing her to the floor. "I said suck me," I bite out harshly.

She sticks out her pink tongue and slowly moves it up and down my length. I close my eyes and revel in the feel of her mouth on my dick. As she clamps her mouth shut over my arousal, I grab a handful of her breast, toying with her nipple until she lets out a low moan. She really does have nice breasts but... I shake my head not wanting to think further. She's finally feeling more confident in her movements, and with my other hand, I push my length to the back of her throat. When she tries to push back, I don't let her.

I'm just starting to get hard until I hear her whimper. I look down at the moisture building along her lashes and pull out, watching her gasp for air. It goes limp once again. Well, that didn't last long. "Sorry sir, I'll try harder," she pants.

When she opens her mouth to try again, I pull back. "You should probably go." My voice is deep and low.

"But... I can try harder," she says while I untie the ropes.

"I'm not interested anymore." It may sound fucked up, but that's the truth. "Go out into the kitchen, I'll meet you there." What she doesn't know is that I'm about to call someone to come pick her up and take her back to the lounge.

"Okay," she says softly as she opens the door and leaves.

I lay down on my bed, frustrated at not being able to have a woman.

"*Kat, Kat, Kat,*" keeps chanting in my head, and I swear I'm going to kill her just to get her out of my system.

"Or you can fuck her," my wolf supplies, not at all helpful. I don't want to touch her at all, but maybe just maybe that can be an option instead of killing her.

Chapter Eight

Kat

Oh...ugh... *"I told you not to answer,"* my wolf chides, and I have to agree with her. I should have ignored it and acted like the message never came through.

Knowing it's her brings a whole new set of questions now. Why does she want the ring? If Theo's planning to marry her, isn't she worth buying a new ring for, not recycling the one he gave to his ex-wife?

Krissy: I want the fucking ring, Kat.

She messages again when I don't respond.

"This bitch needs to calm the fuck down," my wolf says, irritation lacing her every word.

I take it off my finger and twirl it around in my hand, contemplating what to do with it. Deciding that I have no use for it anymore and don't really want it with me, I text her back.

Me: Yeah, sure.

I'm finally free from that relationship. There are no more worries. I've finally moved on.

Krissy: Ok great.

And I can almost hear her fake smile through the phone. I really don't want to see her, but the exchange shouldn't take more than a minute if everything goes well, and she can't really hurt me anymore. The papers are signed, and I feel lighter because of the divorce.

I almost offer up this place but decide against it. This is my home now, and I really don't want her to taint it with her shitty attitude. I always made an effort to be friendly with her because she was Theo's assistant, but she was such a bitch. I guess now I know why there was so much more underneath her friendly smiles. She wanted to get close to Theo. I guess she got what she wanted after all.

Krissy: Do you want to meet up at Theo's house?

Fuck no! But the fact she didn't call it her home doesn't escape my attention.

Me: I'll message you later with directions. We can meet at a halfway point.

This way it'll give me time to look for a place we can meet in the middle.

Krissy: I'm looking forward to it.

Why does it feel like she wants to take something else from me? Like this has to be about more than a ring.

"Because she does," my wolf growls out.

"*Yeah, I guess you're right, at least that will be the last thing that I have from Theo.*" Well, except for the kids, but he won't try to take them away, and I'd put up a fight if he tried.

I put the ring back in its normal place and look at my hand, wondering why I still have the damn thing on my finger. I should've taken it off the day he threw me out. I can't believe it'll be a full week tomorrow since I left the only home I had for so long.

My phone rings. Great, she's trying to call us now. I grab the phone and my heart skips a beat when I see the name on the screen and it's not Krissy.

Dan, why is he calling me? Didn't he get runoff?

I swipe the red button to ignore his call. I no longer trust the guy. He bit me without consent and there's no going back from what he did to me and my kids.

I push him aside and think about the trip instead. The wards are still up so I can't go by myself. They probably put up extra spells, if that's even a possibility because Dan was able to take me out.

The only other person that can take me is Ash unless by some miracle he'll let me go by myself.

My wolf laughs in the background, clearly knowing that won't be an option for me.

Tyler is still indisposed. Benji is obviously not an option. Az is fucking that wolf chick.

Although I'm tempted to knock on the door just to break up what they've got going on, after further thought, I realize that would be kind of fucked up. He'd probably be even pissier with me the whole ride there because he wasn't able to fuck.

Yeah, that's definitely a big no. I go to the office and lift my hand to knock before my knuckles connect with the door. Ash says, "Come in." I open the door and he's there sitting in front of the computer in deep thought. I'm not sure what to do or how to act so I stand there for a long minute. "Are you going to just stand there and watch me like a creeper?"

I scoff, offended. "I'm no creeper." He looks at me, lifting an eyebrow and I roll my eyes at him. "My husband's assistant texted me..."

He scrunches his brows. "Who?" he spits, probably annoyed I interrupted him with something he sees as useless.

"The woman I caught my husband...well ex-husband cheating on me with," I say, correcting myself.

He narrows his eyes with a slight twitch when I call Theo my husband by mistake, and as he focuses all his attention on me, I try not to squirm.

"You better not squirm," my wolf tells me.

"What does she want?" He sounds indifferent, but the way he's looking at me way too closely, I can tell he's invested in this conversation.

If you'd let me finish you would have known by now, is what I want to tell him, but because I need a ride, I have to talk to him nicely. "She wants the ring Theo gave me," I say pleasantly through gritted teeth because it sucks having to act pleasant around him.

"Why does she want the ring?" he asks as if this doesn't make sense to him.

I shrug "Who knows? I didn't ask and I don't really need it, so I don't mind giving it to her."

"Is she coming here?" He sits back in his chair in a relaxed pose, but he's anything but if his stiff shoulders are any indication. It's like he's almost hoping she'd come here so that he can give her the Ash treatment.

"I wouldn't be opposed to that," my wolf pipes up. She's usually always alert when I'm near the guys. When I'm not, she lazily goes back to sleep.

"Actually, no. We're meeting halfway. I found a bar about an hour and a half from here." His face falls slightly, and I know I'm right, he would probably grill her and I can't help but feel a small satisfaction that he'd be on my side. Only briefly because then I get angry that I even want him on my side.

"Well, she's lucky you're being generous. I'd tell her to fuck off then pawn the ring," he says as he looks at my hand. "Why are you still wearing it?" He keeps his face neutral, but I can see it in his eyes. He's been pondering.

"To be honest..." I look down at it, appreciating all the diamonds that adorn the gold band. "I'm not sure." I take it off feeling lighter as if the ring was somehow still bonding me to Theo. I bring it up to my face and smile. "But I'm happy to be getting rid of it."

I feel like a kid asking their parents for permission, and I hate it. I've never had to ask anyone for anything. My foster parents didn't care where I was or where I ended up. "So umm... Can you take me? Or can I go by myself?" My wolf still finds the latter amusing. She knows them a lot better than I do. It must be that she relates to their wolf, and I can't relate to their human side at all. Mostly because these fuckers aren't really human.

"Neither are you." Her voice is filled with amusement.

"Shut up." I wish I could narrow my eyes at her like she does with me.

"Nice comeback," she smirks, only irritating me more.

"I can't take you, and the answer to the next one is a definite no." My face falls. "But I can see if Amara is available," he says in a hopeful voice, and I think that if Amara had plans, he'd make her cancel them just so I'd get rid of the ring.

I nod my head in gratitude. He picks up his cell, scrolling until he finds what he's looking for, and I stand there awkwardly not knowing whether to sit or stand in front of his desk. "Hey, Amara. Kat needs a ride to return the ring from her ex." The way he says the word "ex" is like it leaves a bad taste in his mouth. Theo sure left an impression on him, and it definitely wasn't a good one. "Can you take her?"

"Okay, I'll let her know." He hangs up, never taking his eyes off me.

"She said to meet her upfront in five. You're going straight there and back, no stops anywhere else." This man is so demanding. You could never confuse Ash for being something other than an Alpha. "The only reason I'm letting you go is because Amara has magic and can protect you." Well, it's good to know that I can go places with Amara, maybe I'll bribe her to take me out somewhere for a while. "Do you understand Katarina? Straight there and back," he says in a stern voice, leaving no room for confusion.

"Yes Daddy," I spit, then cringe at my word choice. Shit, that's not what I meant.

He stands still, letting out a low chuckle, and it's the first time I hear that beautiful sound coming out of his mouth. “I see you have a daddy kink.” I wish the floor would swallow me whole. I’m so embarrassed right now.

“I...uh...” I stutter, not knowing how else to play it off.

He saves me by speaking again. “You should throw it out in the woods and make her look for it.” I tilt my head confused. “The ring.”

“He’s got the right idea,” my wolf says.

I giggle nervously before awkwardly hightailing it out of his office.

I’m not sure how I’m going to look him in the eyes after that.

Chapter Nine

Kat

I quickly go to my room and grab the useless piece of metal. I know what Amara said, but it still seems pretty useless to me. Still, I find myself trying to be careful with it when I put it back in my purse.

I have four minutes left, that's enough time to see Benji and Tyler. I immediately go into the medical room. I can't believe this mansion houses a hospital and they have their own personal doctors. I guess you can't have a shifter walking into a human facility. I walk in, and to my surprise, the men are not there. My breath picks up in panic, but then I remember they were going to be moved around noon today and it's already close to one.

I walk out of there wishing I knew where the hospital was. I want to see how they're doing before I leave.

I go outside and there's a red Tesla in front of the house. Amara gives me a small wave to get in. Once I've fallen into the passenger seat, I buckle my seatbelt. I've never been inside a Tesla before, and all I can say is, this is nice. "How's Tyler and Benji doing?" I ask without realizing I didn't greet her or say thank you for driving me. Where are my manners?

She waves her hand away like she knew I felt bad for not even asking her. "Tyler is doing much better, being a shifter helps speed up the healing process, and of course having a strong, powerful witch on your side doesn't hurt." She smiles but it's brief before her face falls and my heart begins pounding hard against my chest. "Benji not so much." Her shoulders hunch in exhaustion.

My eyes pop wide open and I lean closer to her. "Is he going to be alright?" I ask hopeful, still feeling sort of useless that there isn't anything I can do to help.

She sighs, the bags beneath her eyes telling me she's likely been up all night. "It's magic, that's what I know for sure. The doc is using magic to keep Benji alive."

I cross my arms, falling back on my seat and feeling defeated. We're about to cross the border and I hold my breath as if it's going to bounce me back. I hold onto my breath until we're on the other side. Surprisingly nothing happens. Amara gives me a funny look. Well, she would be afraid too if she had bounced back from it like I did.

"We started using magic when we transferred the guys to the hospital." That was probably the time that Az got the call leaving me with his lady friend.

"Does Ash know?" He never mentioned anything, but maybe that's why he was so focused on the screen. Maybe he's looking for a cure or something that can help his brother.

"I called him just before he called me again. I don't think he wanted you stressing out since you have to go see *the assistant*." I laugh at how dramatically she says the word assistant. "Or else he would have told you when you went into his office." She pulls onto the freeway.

"Yeah right," I grumble. "Ash doesn't trust me." If I didn't know any better, I almost sound bitter.

"I wouldn't say that, Kat. He's actually put some trust in you. It's not like him at all." Yeah, I don't believe that story one bit, but I don't want to argue with her. She is doing me a favor after all.

Sensing my hesitance, she begins talking to fill the silence. "So normally with wolves there are some that have mates. Between the ages of sixteen and twenty, you'll feel a tug to go find your mate. With some shifters there are four or more males to one female but sometimes that is not the case, sometimes it's less. From the stories I've heard, if you never feel that tug then you're free to find the person or people you want to be with." Chills run through my body. Why didn't I ever think about them having mates? But knowing this makes my wolf jealous. Like we've already staked our claim and we don't want anyone near them.

"But it doesn't make sense, Ash said he met her." Her mumbles are nearly inaudible. I stay silent because I know there's more to this story, but she doesn't continue with her thoughts.

I listen to her every word since this is all new to me, and I'm trying to figure out what she's getting at. I keep quiet, taking it all in. This information makes no sense. It's like she's trying to piece a puzzle in her head.

The rest of the ride we chat about her life as a witch. She told me she lost a big part of her family when her sister performed black magic. As in, they all died along with three quarters of the witch population. So now their numbers are small. She hasn't seen her sister in so long.

"She was always ambitious. I think she just met the wrong man," she says, gripping the steering wheel tighter.

I can definitely relate to that. I wasn't able to see how controlling Theo was until I got out of the relationship. Then I felt Dan wanted to do the same thing to me. If I didn't meet the guys, I'd probably still be kidnapped by Dan. Switching from one control freak to another.

Az and Ash can be controlling too, but in different ways. I'm betting Az likes to control in the bedroom and Ash likes to control my safety. Theo thrived on controlling my thoughts and behaviors; everything always revolved around him.

Although, I don't think Jess would let that happen to me. I would have found a way to escape Dan's clutches. One way or another, I know for certain that I would have found my freedom.

We exit the freeway, driving through Seattle, I'm a bundle of nerves. Why? I'm not sure. Maybe because the last time I saw this woman she was naked in my bed with Theo.

I twirl the diamond ring playing with it in my hand. I've never taken this off. Probably because I've been wearing it since I was sixteen. I cherished it and viewed it as an extension of my hand.

I know it doesn't mean much as far as marriage is concerned, but I've had the ring for sixteen years of my life. It may not have the meaning that it's supposed to have, but I can't help but feel the loss when it's not on my finger. I didn't think I would. Earlier I felt good about taking it off, but now as this reality sets in, I'm not so sure.

I wish Ash would've let me come by myself, but I get it. I'm a newly turned wolf who doesn't know much about this world, and I have a target on my back. It wouldn't surprise me if Dan tried to snatch me again. That man will not give up.

"You should probably warn the guys he's trying to call you again." Her words turn sour just thinking about Dan.

"Then they'll really keep me locked up in the house." I like my little piece of freedom.

"Don't be ridiculous. They won't do such a thing." She's so sure of herself, and again I'm reminded of how much she trusts them and how my human side is wary of Ash and Az.

"Why is that?"

"Have you met us? As much as we like them, we don't like people telling us what to do. Remember what happened when you found out you couldn't escape. We lost it." I try to argue against *the 'as much as we like them'* part, but it's useless with her. I guess she's right. No one can keep me locked in if I don't want to be.

I also know that the only reason I'm here is because Ash doesn't know Dan tried contacting me. *"We're safe. Amara is driving me, and of course, she has powers that can help us if something goes wrong."*

"Well, you better be right," she says.

"I am," I tell my wolf with confidence.

We find a parking spot right in front of the bar. We got lucky. Usually, it's hard to find any parking around downtown. I look up at the bright red sign that says, Whiskey Bar. The letters k-e-y in the word aren't lighting up anymore. "Oh man, this place looks nasty as fuck, and I really have to pee," she says as she eyes the place in disgust.

I get a notification from Tyler and immediately open my phone. A smile tugs at the corners of my mouth.

Tyler: The magic is helping Benji. We're hoping he'll recover in a few days.

"What is it?" Amara's voice startles me.

"The magic seems to be helping him." My tension releases slightly.

"Oh, thank the goddess." Amara's shoulders loosen.

I look down on my phone typing away.

Me: Yes! Thank you for letting me know. Keep me posted.

Tyler: Always

I open my purse and put my phone inside.

Both of us get out of the car and I look around, making sure we aren't going to get attacked. Maybe coming all the way out here without the guys was a bad idea. I think my paranoia has to do with being kidnapped and thinking someone is going to take me away again.

Upon further inspection of the place, and not seeing very many people surrounding this block, we walk right in.

It smells like mold, cigarettes, and alcohol in here. I want to make this exchange quick. I don't know how much longer I can stand the smell of this place.

It's not very big; it has five booths in the back and five chairs in front of the bar. Definitely not like the Crescent Lounge back home. There aren't very many people here at this time of day. There are four people occupying one booth and three men occupying the booth across the room. The bar is free from many customers and there's no sign of Krissy.

We both walk to the bar and sit on the tall chairs side-by-side. The cushions are hard as fuck. Nothing as comfortable as we have at the Crescent Lounge. "What can I get you, ladies?" The bartender's voice is dark and gravelly. All I want to do is cover my ears, not liking the way his voice sounds.

"I'll take a diet coke," Amara says.

"I'll take a lemonade." The bartender looks at us weird, probably because we're ordering non-alcoholic drinks at a bar. We're not planning on staying long. I'm here on a mission and it's to give Krissy what I no longer need.

"Anything to eat?" I briefly look around, yeah not from the looks of this place.

"Only drinks please." I smile as he huffs and walks away.

"I'll be back, I have to go pee," she says, already getting out of the chair and running to the sketchy bathrooms. I make sure to keep an eye out. I know she can protect herself, but I don't want her caught off guard.

My phone rings, and I pull it out of my purse, looking down at the screen. Fuck, Dan is calling me again. I don't understand why he keeps calling me. Didn't the guys already terrorize him and his pack enough? Clearly, he needs much more than a warning. You'd think he'd get the hint when nearly all the wolves that were with them were killed. If I were him, I wouldn't want to mess with the Iron Beast Pack.

I ignore his call once again and put the phone back in my purse.

"I don't have a good feeling about this," my wolf says as I discreetly look around the area, noting all the exits. *"Keep your eyes sharp."* My breath picks up. Is it just me or is everyone at this bar staring at me now? It's like they stopped chatting and I've become the center of attention. I keep an eye out where Amara went to make sure no one is getting up to go to the bathroom.

I hold on to my purse tightly. Nope, we're not staying. I'm about to get up when someone sits right beside me. My body stiffens and I smell a slightly pungent smell. That's familiar but more intense now with my wolf nose. I look up. Oh, that's why.

My wolf wants to growl as Krissy comes close to me.

"Let's not make a scene," I tell my wolf. I'm on the verge of shifting, and all I want to do is give her what she came for and leave this place and never come back. She looks professional with a high waisted black pencil skirt, black heels, and a bright red satin shirt that compliments her skin color. Her hair is perfectly styled in loose waves, and she's wearing heavy makeup with red lipstick. She looks more out of place than I do even with my jeans and casual shirt. She really is beautiful, but I still hate her for what she did to me. Although maybe I should thank her. She did save me from having to spend the rest of my life with Theo.

She's all smiles as she slides into Amara's chair next to me, but it's a smile that doesn't quite reach her dull, charcoal eyes. "Hey Kat." I flinch at the acid in her tone and her dry grin has me shivering. I'm not sure why she hates me so much, you'd think I was the one who stole her husband.

Having stashed the ring in my purse on the way over, I dive inside my bag, not trying to be here longer than necessary. My hand brushes against the Kiss of Death, and a shiver rolls through me. Even though I don't know how to use it, having it with me makes me feel a little safer.

Before pulling the ring out, I look around the bar, expecting the men across the room to be watching us still. I really don't trust the shady guys day drinking in a seedy bar like this one, but they have all gone back to what they were doing before we walked in. They look stiffer than they should, though, and my gut tells me something is wrong.

The sooner I get out of here, the better.

When I find the ring, I pull it out and give it to her. "Here you go," I say as the bartender slams our drinks down in front of me, and my eyes fly back to the table closest to us. I refuse to get jumped for this stupid ring, if those men try to take it, they can have it. It's not worth risking our lives for.

I briefly think about what Ash said, to throw it out and make her look for it, and as amusing as that sounds, I decide to be an adult about this and open my palm. She snatches it immediately, holding it to the light, inspecting it. She doesn't care that there are men surrounding us, but my paranoia has me on edge. "I didn't change the diamonds," I say slightly annoyed, thinking that's why she's holding it up to the light.

She closes her palms while she smiles at me and opens it back up. "Nah, I don't want it anymore." She snatches my wrist back, and damn she has a tight grip. She pushes the rings back into my hand.

"I'll just have Theo give me something flashier." I bite my tongue hard trying to be civil about this, but I imagine myself punching her in the face and making her bleed.

"I bet Az would like that," my wolf chuckles darkly.

I'm startled when Az pops into my head. These men have really ingrained themselves in my every thought. Which brings out the fury that I've been feeling from everything that's happened this past week. "Are you saying you made me come all the way here, demanded that I give you this damn ring, and now you don't want it anymore?" My voice is low but full of anger. I couldn't leave the irritation out of it. I guess fuck being civilized.

As if it doesn't faze her, she rises from the chair. "Yeah Kat, that's not worth my time." I see red, or maybe that's my wolf vision. I look away so that she won't notice my eyes changing color. I keep looking down, avoiding eye contact with anybody else. I face the bathroom, wondering why Amara is taking so long. I never watched anybody trying to pry the door open, so I'm sure no one went in there after her.

Once I'm calm enough and I know my eyes have changed back, I grab her hand. "Here, just give it back to Theo." She pulls away before I can touch her, and I stare at her retreating figure in shock.

She moves quickly toward the door, and unless I want to get in a fight—which is tempting—all I do is watch her leave. "It's not worth his time either," she spits, pulling her sunglasses over her eyes and pushing through the exit.

"What just happened?" I say to my wolf.

"Well, it looks like that ungrateful bitch was hoping for bigger diamonds." My wolf is annoyed.

"Kat, what's wrong?" Amara startles me away from the door, and I turn to face her, only she's not looking at me, she's looking at everyone else at the bar. She grabs my hand. "Come on, we need to go." Her eyes are wary, her lips tight in a grimace.

I stand up to leave when the bartender comes closer. "Why don't you ladies have your drinks?" Warning alarms go off inside my head, and my body slightly trembles in fear.

We're in big trouble.

Chapter Ten

Kat

I look at the drinks we ordered, they're just sitting right in front of us, and my stomach turns at the thought of drinking it.

"No thank you," Amara says. "We should probably get going." She grabs my arm harder to drag me toward the door. She doesn't have to put in much effort because I'm going willingly. There are two bald guys standing in front of the door blocking our escape, and there's nothing friendly about them.

"Have a drink and relax," the bartender insists, and I'm starting to believe that he might have added a little something else to what we ordered. An extra kick. I'm certain he wants to drug us.

"You should listen to Jim," a guy sitting by the booth says. I'm assuming Jim is the bartender, and I already know it's a hell no from us.

My wolf starts to creep out from her cave. She wants blood. We're backed into a corner, and she doesn't like that very much.

I don't notice when my eyes change colors, but I hear a few of them gasp. One of them laughs louder. "Oh, girl." He points at me with a long, shaky finger. "You better watch out, they'll be coming for you." So, they are supernaturals. I really need to learn how to tell if someone is human or not. "You..." He doesn't get to finish before I shift into a wolf, shredding all my clothes, and running at full speed, taking a huge chunk off his neck.

The other one is more aware of what I'm trying to do. He hits the side of my face, and I go down, sliding to the other side of the bar. I hear Amara say an incantation, or at least I think it is. It's quickly confirmed when the bartender goes up in flames, but she gets hit from behind and goes down.

I try to run after her when one of them grabs me by the neck, putting a knee on my body so I won't move. He gets close to my face. "You're definitely a prize," he says in my ear. "I can't wait to take you home." No, no, no. Thoughts of being kidnapped again start rising. My body is going into full panic mode, and my vision blurs. No, I can't let that happen to me again.

"You need to shift, Kat," my wolf urges me in an uneasy tone, which has my body in full on fear while trying to get out of his tight hold. Fuck, I'm going to be naked.

I grit my teeth together, nostrils flaring, but I can't move. How the hell am I going to shift? I close my eyes, trying to shut off everything around me so maybe I can concentrate on turning back. It isn't as hard or as bad as when I turned into a new wolf, but I still need to concentrate to be able to do it.

I'm already losing my mind a little bit because I've killed a person. They're probably not human, but it doesn't make it any less difficult. A life is a life. That's something I thought I'd never do. They probably have families.

"Don't go there," my wolf growls at me. *"If you do. You'll lose your shit, and we can't have that."* My wolf is absolutely right. I push it off to the side and lock it in a box that I won't open for a long while.

When I hear a high-pitched scream, I open my eyes back up to see what's going on, but my view is blocked by another man. They're doing something to Amara.

"Change now!" my wolf yells. The demand in her voice activates the change in me. As my body adjusts to human, his arm falters, and that's all I need to get out of his hold, punching the guy the same way I wanted to punch Krissy earlier.

"Grab your weapon!" Amara shouts.

I stop for a moment. "That useless thing?" I blurt out, puzzled as to what the hell that piece of shit is going to do for us. Am I supposed to chuck it at them and they'll go down? Not wanting to waste any more time, I run back to the bar in all my naked glory, noticing that Amara is pinned between two males.

I look around the bar quickly, trying to find my purse, and when I spot it on a nearby chair, I rip it open and grab the Kiss of Death with shaking hands. "What the hell am I supposed to do with this now?" I'm about to shake it when I feel a tremble in the palm of my hand. The metal feels warm as it grows to fit my grip, and a sharp purple tip comes out of the hole, expanding like a telescoping knife.

Whoa.

I turn around with it, and when the guys see me, they slowly start to back away, keeping a tight hold on Amara. I run at an alarming speed toward the two men holding Amara, and they finally show some fear in their eyes. I can almost taste how scared they are. In one swift movement, and without thinking, I shove the purple blade against the one that's turned away from me and stab him. Not enough to kill him...I think.

Nope, I was wrong. The man wails in pain, turning over and letting Amara go. Fuck, when he turns over, his shirt is slightly torn from the wound, and it looks bad, really bad.

I hold the Kiss of Death in my hand with wide eyes, staring at it like it's a threat. "What in the hell was that?" I question out loud.

The rest of the men back away, and the man holding Amara raises his hands slowly, releasing her and edging toward the door.

"I told you that's a powerful weapon," she pants from the floor. I extend my hand to help her up and see a huge gash on the corner of her scalp. "It will heal." She looks at my worried gaze. "Just take me to the car. You're going to have to drive us back."

I nod, pulling a tablecloth from one of the booths and wrapping it around my body. As we sidestep the men I just killed, I grab our purses from the bar, trying not to think about what happened. If I do, I'm sure I'll fall to pieces.

I open the car with shaky hands and gently help her into her seat. She grabs her phone and immediately dials a number, but I don't have to ask, I already know who she's calling.

"You guys need to get someone to clean up the mess at the Whi—" She doesn't finish before she pauses again. "Yeah, she's alive." She listens to the other end of the call when I go around to the driver's side, trying to tune out the voices. My hands are still shaking, but I know I need to calm down before I can drive. "We'll tell you about it when we get home."

She puts her phone down. “Be ready when we get home, Ash is losing his shit right now. He said no pit stops and to come straight home,” she says, closing her eyes. Fuck, I have to face Ash after calling him Daddy. This is going to be awkward as hell. I’m going to die of embarrassment. “Hey, did the homewrecker ever show up?” She thankfully breaks my current dilemma, but I’m not sure I like this new conversation.

I almost forgot that was the whole reason we went there. “Yeah,” I laugh, but there’s no humor to it. “She didn’t want it.” I grip the steering wheel a little harder than I should.

“Huh?” She lifts a perfectly waxed brow at me, and I wonder if she gets her eyebrows done or if she uses magic to get them to look that perfect.

“Apparently, the diamonds are too small for her liking,” I remember when he first gave it to me, I thought it had the biggest diamonds I’d ever seen.

She snorts. “Wow, she must be a piece of work.” She laughs nervously, and I know it’s because of what we went through. “If we could make a pit stop, I would tell you to sell the ring, but that will have to wait until we figure out what the hell went wrong today.”

Once I’ve merged onto the freeway, I glance sideways at Amara in the passenger seat with her legs pulled up to her chest. “Why did you take so long in the bathroom?" Remembering she was out for the whole encounter.

She rests her head back. "That toilet was nasty." She shivers in disgust. "I had to sanitize everything." I don't ask her any more questions, but I'm glad I didn't have to go.

"Oh, I almost forgot." Her voice is weak and tired. I wonder how much magic she used. She grabs her purse from the backseat. "I got you a belt for your weapon and a strap so you can hide it under your clothes."

"Thank you." My heart tugs at her kindness. Maybe she'll be alright after all. What I'm not looking forward to is getting bombarded with questions by Ash.

Chapter Eleven

Tyler

I'm waiting outside on the front porch for Kat to come home, wondering what the hell happened out there. I shouldn't be out here like this, exposed to threats. I'm still weakened by what went on with Benji. Doc said he didn't advise me to leave his care because I'm supposed to be resting. Of course, he can't really make me do anything I don't want to do. I'm an Alpha, and although he's the doc and should be treated with as much respect, I did use my status to get away.

I know I'll have to apologize later, but I've been on pins and needles since Ash called me and told me Kat and Amara ran into trouble. I should've gone with her and been there protecting her. My wolf is pacing around relentlessly waiting for her return. My wolf has claimed her as his. We know it's not a true bond, but this is the person we want to spend the rest of our life with. It's as if we've been waiting for her our whole life.

We already have guys at the bar looking to see who the fuck messed with our woman, and once we figure it out, they'll have hell to pay.

I keep chewing on my thumbnail, counting down the minutes until she's by my side. Ash is locked in his office, no doubt staring at the camera we have on our front door. I can almost feel his hard stare through the lens. Az is in his room watching the camera through his phone. I know that I should be doing something useful on the computer to try and find out if I can ID those guys, but I can't think at the moment, at least not until I have her safely in my arms.

I hear tires driving through the forest just as the car comes into sight, and before they have the chance to fully stop, I'm already running toward the car. I open the door to the driver's side and nearly yank Kat from the seat, immediately grabbing her and keeping her tight in my arms.

Ash is already here. I knew his whole focus was on the camera. A spark of concern flashes through his eyes and then it's gone. He's heading straight to Amara, but his eyes wander over to Kat.

"Are you okay, Kat?" I ask, finally noticing she's wearing a cream-colored tablecloth. Ash and I both hold our breaths impatiently waiting for her to talk.

"Yeah. I'm just happy to be home," she says, biting her bottom lip and looking down at the ground, but I have a feeling much more went on. Maybe she's not ready to talk about it, but I'll be here when she is.

"Home." My wolf likes the taste of the word that came out of her mouth. I agree with my other half. I want her to feel like this is her home too because well, it is now.

"Can I stay with you for a while?" she asks shyly, giving me a hopeful stare. I know she doesn't want to be alone.

I smile down at her. "Of course, you can, but I have to give you a heads up, I'll be on the computer trying to see if I can find any information on the attack."

"I love it when you get all nerdy," she says, kissing me on the lips. I fist her hair, wanting her to open more, and she obliges.

"Get a room," Az snaps, looking irritated as he walks past us. He clearly hasn't had sex and is taking it out on us. I let myself chuckle at his misery.

I grab her hand and pull her inside the house. I practically drag her to my room and slam the door shut, pinning her against the wall. Her eyes widen with excitement. "I like this side of you, Tyler."

I get closer to her again, claiming her mouth and loving her sweet taste of cherries. I want more, but I pull back before it gets any further. She reluctantly lets go with a slight pout.

"I want to take this further, Kat." I lean my head against hers. "But I need to figure out who tried to hurt you." Our mouths are close together, and I'm tempted to kiss those rosy lips again but pull away before I take her to bed and get nothing done.

"I get it," Kat says. "I need to go shower anyway." She looks around her body in disgust, and I get the feeling she wants to be alone for a moment. "I need to..." It's as if she's looking at herself for the first time. She didn't notice the blood that was on her until now. "I need to scrub myself." I nod my head. When she comes back in, I'll make sure to ask her what happened.

She reluctantly leaves the room and I close the door. I know it must not have been easy for her to do what she did but I'm glad she didn't second guess herself.

I get comfortable in my chair, and as soon as I try to log in to the computer, Ash barges in without knocking.

I look up from the computer. "Did she say what happened?" He looks around the room as if he'll find her hiding in the corner, but I think he purposely waited until Kat went into her own room. His timing was impeccable.

"She hasn't said much, but she needed a bit of time to process things." I type in my password and my computer screen flickers up.

"Amara told me she has a weapon." I stop what I'm doing, giving him my full attention. "It's the Kiss of Death." My eyes widen. "Not just any dagger, Tyler. It's dangerous, even to us." If this is true, we need to make sure it doesn't touch us; we could die instantly.

"But how?" I ask baffled that this is happening. "Didn't the family line that could wield the weapon die?" From what I remember they've all been killed off.

He shrugs. "I'm as surprised as you are." I knew that she needed to be protected from the council, but now it seems like she's going to need protection from others as well.

"How's Amara doing?" I ask, remembering that I didn't even acknowledge her existence when she came back. I just grabbed Kat and took her upstairs to my room. I was a man on a mission to try and get my girl to safety.

"Amara is okay. A little banged up but healing as we speak." He rubs his chin in thought, and I know he has more to say. "Did Katarina tell you?"

"Tell me what?" I have a feeling low in my gut that I'm not going to like where this is going.

"The girl never took the ring," he says as he drags one hand across his platinum hair. The only indication he's irritated for Kat. I don't see why Ash doesn't want to admit he cares for her. I know it has something to do with meeting our mate and her being killed right before his eyes, but I wish he could move on—we have. But maybe I can't fault him too much. It'd probably be a lot harder to move on if I remembered her face, her smell, her eyes.

"Task at hand," my wolf growls at me, obviously upset on our girl's behalf. I'm actually surprised because my wolf never felt anything for the woman that died. Sure, we felt bad, but it wasn't as heart breaking as I imagined. I don't quite know if that makes me a bad person.

Coming back to our conversation, I focus on my brother's troubled scowl. "Are you fucking serious? She made Kat drive all the way to the bar only for her not to want the ring?" I feel angry on Kat's behalf because she's been through the wringer with that woman. Watching her as she fucked her ex couldn't be easy to witness. Personally, I would have killed them both right then and there. I think that's what makes me a part of this pack. I can be nice, but when I switch gears, I can be ruthless. It wasn't easy to try and be civilized in front of Theo, but I was thinking about Kat and her kids. Even if Benji and I are the calm ones when it comes to Kat and her kids, there is something inside of us that wants to unleash itself when we see them hurt.

"Apparently, the diamonds were too small," he says in a neutral voice, but I know him well enough to know when he's pissed. The nerve of this woman. I'm not one to be rude, but I know if I ever met her, I'd give her a piece of my mind. "Let me know if you find anything," he says as he closes the door.

I get back online looking through all the cameras around the Seattle area, trying to figure out if anybody arrived at the bar around the same time. I go through every snippet of footage and hack every camera within reach, but every damn shot looks the same. I get closer to the monitors trying to see if I can spot anything, but every single camera is identical.

I sit back in my chair to think this through. They knew I'd track the cameras, so someone had to have covered their tracks. Nothing was recorded during the times I'm trying to check. It started recording again an hour after they left, and it stopped recording just before they arrived.

Clearly, this was planned, but by who and why?

My body is nearing exhaustion, but a shot of adrenaline hits me, and I sit up. "Shit, Kat's phone has been hacked," I say out loud to the empty room. It's the only explanation on why the cameras were shut down for a specific amount of time. There was no maintenance being done.

I immediately grab my phone and dial Az's number; he picks up on the first ring. "On your way back to the house, can you get Kat and the kids new phones? Kat's phone has been hacked and I'm sure the kids have been too." Even if theirs wasn't hacked, there is a big possibility that they could have been, and I'd rather play it safe and assume that theirs are compromised too.

"Sure thing brother. Anything else?" he says way too casually, but I know him and the code he uses to indirectly ask how Kat is doing. He's worried. I debate whether to let him stew a little longer to see if he'll eventually ask about her, but he's just as stubborn as Ash.

I decide to be a good brother and put him out of his misery. "She seems okay for now. I'll talk to her after her shower to see how she's really doing."

There's nothing for a moment until he sighs as if he were holding his breath and waiting for the news. "Okay, I'll let Benji know." I don't want to push him further by making fun of him for not asking about Kat directly. He's already on edge with everything going on, plus no sex, that's not a good combination.

After hanging up with Az, I go to Kat's room and grab her phone from the dresser, and just as she walks out of the shower wrapped in a towel, I smash it.

She has a puzzled expression, her brows dipping low on her face with a slight frown. "What did the phone ever do to you?"

"You were being tracked." Her mouth is wide open in shock. "That's how they knew where you'd be at the bar. I bet anything that they were waiting for you to leave the property so they could follow you."

"Well—that's unsettling," she mumbles.

"I'll let you get dressed. Az is bringing you and the kids new phones."

"Thank you," she mumbles without argument. I think she'd rather be safe, even if that means we have to purchase new phones for them. Or maybe it's something else. She turns away before I can decipher what that look is.

I probably just imagined it. I've been on edge with everything that's been going on. At least that emergency is out of the way. I watch the water droplets running down the strands of her dark hair, and there's a low grumble from deep in my stomach.

"Don't tease me, Tyler." Her voice is breathy, and I can already smell her arousal mingling with mine. Her pretty brown eyes change to violet as she gazes longingly at me.

I'm tired and weak but I want her so badly. Thinking something happened to her earlier left me with so much exhaustion.

She drops her towel. "Oops," she says with a saucy smirk.

Fuck it. She smiles like she's won, but she knows I want this as bad as she does. She crawls across the bed, positioning herself in the middle with her elbows propped up, watching me take off my clothing in record time.

She slides her bottom lip through her teeth, her eyes are on my hardening length. I pump my hand up and down a few times as Kat watches me. "Stop it, Kat. You're going to make me come and I haven't even been inside of you yet," I growl out.

"Well, bring that fine beast over here." I chuckle and do as she commands. Fuck it, I know what I said earlier, but I want her here and now.

She lays on her bed while I meet her there, grabbing her thighs and pulling them apart. I breathe in her sweet cherry scent, knowing I will never get tired of the way it draws me in.

I kiss her gently, and as my mouth hovers over her skin, my canines push out.

"Bite her." I have to stop myself, surprised that the thought came to my mind. *"Make her ours, permanently."*

"No. It doesn't work that way, you know that." My wolf stirs inside of me saying something else, but I quiet that part of my mind and focus on my woman.

She pushes her sweet pussy in my face as if reminding me why the hell I'm between her legs. I chuckle darkly and give her what she's been waiting for. She moans and fists her pillow as I lick through her folds, grabbing a handful of her tit and rolling her round pebble into pretty brown peaks.

"Bite her," he says more forcefully. He's trying to persuade me while I'm lost in a cloud of lust.

"If you don't stop, I won't let you out for a week." With that, he finally stays quiet, and I go back to focusing on Kat.

With my other hand, I thrust two fingers, pumping in and out slowly to match the rhythm of my tongue. "Tyler, you need to do this to me every fucking day," she groans, and my cock twitches at the sight of her coming undone with the pleasure I'm giving her.

"Please, Tyler," she pleads. I thrust a third finger, and this time I make my movements faster.

"I'm going to come," she yells out, twisting the sheets in her fists. I push my cock into her, riding her wave. Her walls clench and I almost spill my seed right then and there. I have to stop moving for a second, and when I know I'm not going to combust, I move again. The last of her orgasm finishes, and I don't take it easy on her. I ravage her pussy. I was scared out of my mind that something might have happened to her, and I have a lot of pent-up energy to release.

She holds onto both sides of my arms, squeezing them gently. I look into her eyes. There's so much love there, my heart hurts.

What I don't understand is why this woman isn't my mate. Why did it have to be someone else?

"I love you, Tyler." It's the first time I've heard those words from a woman that I care so deeply for, and in this moment, I know I'm never going to let her go.

"Nope. Never." My wolf agrees.

"I love you too, Kat." As I say those words to her, my cock swells up while she squeezes me tightly. I lower my body and kiss her as we both ride our release.

When I've finally come down from the high, I lay down next to her. She's still panting but has a huge smile. Those words mean everything to her, as they do to me.

I take a moment to reassess my body, and it's like she's renewed my energy. I no longer feel tired but more energetic and ready to take on the day. Well, it's night now.

We fall asleep on her bed. I don't remember drifting off until it's five in the morning the next day.

I slowly get up from the bed, but she stirs awake. "Tyler." Her voice is groggy. "Where are you going this late?"

"It's actually early, love." *Love,* because I love her.

She sits up quickly, almost like someone poured cold water over her head. "Really?" She looks outside but it's pitch black and then she checks her phone. "Huh?" She stares up at me with a grin. "That sex put you to sleep," she giggles.

"I have to go, but I would rather stay with you." I want to hang out with her, but I have work to do, so I begrudgingly get up from the bed and get dressed slowly. Kat props herself up on one elbow, watching me put on my clothes. "Kat, you can't be looking at me like that or else I'm not leaving this room."

"I wouldn't be opposed to that." She bites her lip and I have to turn away from her naked body.

"If I didn't have shit to do, I'd be all over you." I grab my shoes and put them on, then lean back across the bed to kiss her gently. She tastes so sweet.

"Come check on me later," I tell her as I pull away. She nods and I go to the door, closing it as I leave.

There's a call on my phone from Doc. I swipe the green button and put it to my ear, but before I can greet him, he starts talking. "Tyler," he says urgently, and the good mood I was feeling just moments ago vanishes. "I need you here. Amara will explain everything when you arrive. Benji is dying."

Chapter Twelve

Kat

It's Monday morning, my kids should be heading downstairs soon. I still have the phones Az brought me sometime last night. They're probably eagerly waiting for me to bring them theirs.

Az comes barging into my room, I barely have time to cover my body. "I had the kids give me their phones last night. I told them I bought them new ones and left them with you. But I locked the door so they wouldn't come in while Tyler was sleeping here." Well, that's very considerate of him since I haven't told the kids we're dating yet. I have no clue how that conversation will go.

Before I can say anything else, he walks out of the room like he has better things to do. I must say, I'm glad to see Az's face instead of Ash. I'm still feeling a little embarrassed at calling him Daddy.

I'm updating my phone when I get a call from Dan. He's relentless. He keeps calling my phone nonstop. I swipe ignore again. I don't think I'll ever be able to talk to him the same way I used to. Once you lose my trust, there is no coming back from it.

As I'm trying to block his number, a message comes in.

"Don't," my wolf chides. *"Remember what happened the last time I told you to ignore a message and you didn't listen to me,"* she warns.

I remember clearly.

I know I shouldn't. I really do know better. But—curiosity takes over and I open the message.

My wolf stomps angrily to her corner.

Dan: Have your men told you they've worked for the council? The same people that want you killed.

Umm... Shit, no they haven't. I wasn't expecting this revelation so early in the morning. My hand trembles as I hold tightly to my phone.

Dan: They killed people for them and they're going to kill you too.

No, that can't be right. He's lying. Why would they go to all the trouble driving three hours just so they can come get me and my kids? They had other more important matters that were going on, yet they still came. Surely they wouldn't take me and provide a place for us to live just to kill me.

My fingers hover over the keyboard. *"Don't do it,"* my wolf yells at me. I bite my lip hard. *"Nothing good will come of this."* I know she's right, but they need to tell him off overtakes any logic.

Me: You don't know what you're talking about Dan.

But the argument sounds weak.

"You should have left it alone. He's planted the seed of doubt and now he knows it." I know what my wolf means, but I want to prove him wrong, or maybe I'm trying to prove to myself that he's wrong.

Dan: I know someone that can help you. That can help us escape. Didn't you say they practically held you hostage?

I scrunch my eyebrows. How does he know about that? I was going to message him back to ask him, but he continues.

Dan: I know that I haven't been forthcoming but I didn't want to scare you.

Me: You should've been forthcoming before you bit me.

I bite back as I type those letters angrily. I'm surprised I didn't break the screen with the extra strength of a shifter coursing through me.

Me: But whatever, it's done I can't go back to being a human.

"If you ever were?" My wolf says to me, and I have to close my eyes and take a calming breath. Maybe I was never fully human, but that notion frightens me. I thought not knowing who my parents were was bad enough, but now realizing I might have been a different species altogether scares me. What will come of it with my kids?

Dan: We could be so good together Kat. Only if you let me. I can be better than Theo and clearly better than the four men you're with.

I swallow hard through a thick lump in my throat. *"Just end it now before it gets worse for us."* I have to agree with her. I can't let this conversation go any further.

Me: Well, it was nice talking to you. Please don't contact me ever again.

I press send and go back to trying to figure out how to block his ass before another message comes through, but it's already on the screen and my eyes lock onto his words.

Dan: I bet Benji is in bad shape now. Isn't he?

My wolf is as attentive as I am right now, my finger hovering over the block button.

I was going to ask how he knew about that, but it's no use. My phone was tampered with. He could have listened in somehow. The same way he knew I felt like I was being trapped in this house.

Me: He's recovering now. First to recover is Tyler and soon it will be Benji.

I message back as I'm remembering what Tyler and I did right before he had to ruin my bliss.

Dan: Is he now?

My blood turns cold, and I nearly drop the phone. Is he messing with me again? Because he's doing a good job having me second guess everything.

Dan: Well, if something suddenly goes wrong, I have something that can help.

I can just imagine his smirk through the other side of the phone. I used to think it looked handsome on him, now I fucking hate it.

I don't like the way that sounds. I need to go check on Benji, even if only to give myself peace of mind.

Walking downstairs to meet the kids, I find the house cook already at work. "Good morning, Lily." I try to sound cheerful, but I don't have the energy anymore.

"Good morning, Kat. Have you heard from Benji?" she asks, clearly worried. "I haven't seen Tyler, Az, or Ash."

"I was with Tyler this morning, but he left. I'm not sure where." She shakes her head in relief. I don't dare mention what Dan said to me. He's probably trying to scare me.

"I have to get some groceries, but I'll be back later." I wave at her as she leaves through the kitchen door.

My kids come in through the opposite side of the door. “Mom,” Ezra says. “Where are our new phones?

“No good morning?” I roll my eyes.

“Sorry, Mom. Good morning,” Ezra comes up and hugs me. “But about the phone.” I pull them out of my pocket and hand one to each of them.

“Oh my God!” Ava exclaims. “This is the new iPhone” she jumps up and down. “I’m going to thank Az when I see him.”

“Nice.” Ezra looks just as excited as he inspects it.

There’s a car pulling up. “Oh, gotta go.” Ava gives me a kiss on one side of my cheek before leaving while Ezra tackles the other side. They both grab a granola bar and a piece of fruit on their way out.

This time I pull out my phone and call Tyler, but there’s no answer. It goes to voicemail. I try once more with the same result. I go back upstairs and open the door, walking straight into his room, but it’s empty. My stomach drops. The room is the way I left it when I showered. He should have been here. That’s what he told me only a couple of hours ago.

Swallowing my pride, I dial Ash’s number. I don’t bother with niceties. “Where are you keeping Benji? I haven’t seen him since before he was moved to the hospital.”

He clears his throat before answering, and I know nothing good will come out of his mouth. I can smell his fear from the phone. “Kat, maybe you shouldn't see him. He's not... He's not doing well." I feel as if someone is leaning up against my chest making it hard to breathe as soon as those words leave his mouth. I need to see him even more now. There's nothing that's going to keep me from seeing him.

I forget all about being embarrassed yesterday, focusing on the way his words come out like he's saddened by what's going on. I don't like this one bit. "I want to see him now." I use my mom voice. It's demanding and holds no room for argument.

He sighs like he won't argue with me about this. "I'll take you there later this evening." My jaw drops. What the hell am I going to do until then?

"I know what you're thinking, Katarina, but they won't even let me in there." He exhales harshly, and I can picture him blowing a long ribbon of smoke from his lips the way he does when he's losing control. "You're probably not going to work this week." Before I can argue he says, "I have to go. I'll call you back when I'm able to take you. Don't think about calling Az right now, he's in a mood." He hangs up before I even get a chance to ask about Tyler.

Standing outside of Tyler's room, I'm not sure what I'm supposed to do. I usually work at night, but during the day I'm able to do whatever I want.

"How about going into the Jacuzzi?" my wolf offers.

I shrug. *"We can do that. We need some time to ourselves and relax."* Although I'm not sure how much I'll be able to relax knowing that Benji isn't doing so great.

I go back to my room and find a black and red bikini with cherries on it in one of my drawers. When I slide it on, I look at myself in the mirror, really admiring the tattoo on my torso.

I walk downstairs taking my towel, phone, and some water with me. I look at the huge pool, thinking about all of the parties they probably host here. As I climb into the biggest Jacuzzi I've ever seen, my muscles relax as the hot water rises to my shoulders.

I can't completely ease my mind since it wanders to Benji and what Dan said about the guys working for the council, the same people that want to see me dead.

I look out into the forest. *"Hey, wolf."* She perks up from the lazy sleeping position she's in.

"What?" she answers angrily.

"You want to go out for a run?" She perks up at that. *"I'll take that as a yes,"* I chuckle. I haven't let her free in a while and running is her way to destress.

I grab my phone from the chair and try to call Jess, but she doesn't pick up.

Me: Call me when you get the chance. I miss you.

I stay here for another hour, appreciating the landscape that surrounds the property. The backyard is set up with outdoor tables and chairs. There's a huge gazebo with mosaic tiles equipped with a BBQ, a smoker, and two big fireplaces. I need to hang out here more often. Then of course there are the huge trees that surround the house.

I finally get out and grab my towel from where it's laying over one of the lounge chairs. I dry myself off realizing that I don't really need to do that since I'll be shifting.

The area seems desolate, and even though I have an odd feeling that someone is watching me, I know I'm just being paranoid. I quickly take off my swimsuit and let my bones readjust until I'm on all fours.

We run for hours, only stopping a couple of times at the lake before continuing on. I find more houses that I didn't even know were here. The people that live there see me but leave me alone. This would be hard to do in the city. I'm so glad we have this place to let loose and enjoy nature.

I make my way back to the yard and shift to human form, grabbing the already dry towel and putting it around me. I check my phone for messages. Nothing from Jess or Tyler, but there is one from Ash. My heart skips a beat before opening it.

Ash: Meet me outside in thirty minutes.

I panic a moment, checking to see when it was sent, and it looks like it was only five minutes ago. Seeing that I have time to spare, I grab my bathing suit and water bottle, cracking the lid and drinking it on the way upstairs to get dressed.

Ash is already outside in the driveway smoking a cigarette when I find my way back downstairs. Does he ever not smoke? On anyone else, it would disgust me, but on him, the scent of tobacco with its hint of woody and sweet vanilla makes him more attractive. "Let's go."

"It's because he's ours, anything he does will look attractive on him," she voices from her corner.

"We're walking?" I look out into the distance. "Shouldn't we take a car?" I ask, granted I have no idea where it is or if you need a car to get there. No wait, that would be pretty dumb if you couldn't get there without a car since it's a hospital.

"No, I need the fresh air. We can run." Well, that doesn't sound too fun, but I'm down for it anyway. The urge to see him is overriding my senses.

He puts out the cigarette, throwing it in the ashtray, and before he says anything, he's sprinting away. I follow closely behind, but he's still too fast for me. "Come on, Kat," he shouts looking back. "You're too fucking slow." Wanting to prove him wrong, I pump my legs faster and faster until I catch up to him. My muscles are on fire and my breathing is heavier.

This is the first time he looks so carefree. Being outside really brings out a different person in him. Someone who's not so uptight, and I briefly wonder what this side of him is like. He laughs at my struggle, but not like he's making fun of me, more like he's impressed by how hard I'm pushing to beat him.

I see a white building approaching. I'm almost there. I can feel him right behind me. My hand touches the wall. Oh my gosh, I think I beat him here. That euphoric feeling doesn't last long because I'm reminded that I'm here for a reason. Benji.

I open the door to the building. This place looks like a doctor's office and hospital at the same time. "Hi, you must be Kat," the lady at the front desk greets me. She wears a sad smile and the good mood I had moments ago vanishes.

Something is wrong. I can sense it.

We follow the lady to the back where there are two beds. My face pales and my hands get clammy as I approach the one closest to me.

Benji looks dead. "What the fuck happened?" There's a slight tremble in my voice. I sniff and touch my face and my hand comes away wet with tears.

"We thought he was going to be fine, but things took a turn for the worse." A gentleman wearing a white lab coat speaks up. I didn't see him when

I walked in, so he must have just shown up or I must not be paying attention to my surroundings. He looks to be in his early thirties.

There's a low growl coming from Ash. "Oh, calm down, Ash. I'm not going to ask Kat out on a date." He glares at Ash, but then he turns to look at me sympathetically, and I can't tell if it's because I have to deal with Ash for the rest of my life or because he knows I have a relationship with Benji or maybe both. "I'm Dr. Jones, it's very nice to meet you, Kat. I just wish it were under different circumstances." I nod my head agreeing with the man.

Someone else grabs my attention. "Who's on the other—" Oh shit, what the fuck? I walk past the doctor and go to the next bed. "What happened to Tyler?" I saw him not so long ago and he was doing just fine. Well, maybe a bit exhausted, but part of that was my fault. No wait, he looked more energized after we had sex, but Tyler looks so drained now.

"We needed one of the Alpha's powers to help stabilize him." Amara comes in looking more worn out since I saw her yesterday. Damn, what happened? Everyone looks like death.

"And Tyler volunteered before Az and I got here," Ash says, looking more exhausted than usual.

"We need to figure out a cure fast or they won't make it through the week." Shit, this is not what I wanted to hear.

Chapter Thirteen

Kat

Dan knew this would happen.

But how? Does he have someone on the inside feeding him information?

My heart beats faster. "I have to go." I tell them abruptly. I need to get out of here before I give myself away. Amara lifts her brow in confusion but doesn't ask any questions. She either thinks I'm crazy or that I need time to process what's going on with my men. Ash looks at me like he knows something is wrong, and knowing him, he won't let this go. I'll answer his questions after I get what I need.

I close the door before anybody can say anything and sprint to the house, taking the stairs two at a time all the way to my room and grabbing a backpack from the closet. I stuff some extra clothing in there and grab my dagger and strap from my purse. I look at it, wondering how the hell I got so lucky to have this.

The phone in my back pocket feels heavier than it should, and with every anxious step around the room, I debate on what to do next. I can't ignore what Dan said anymore. If Benji and Tyler die—no I can't think this way. If there's a slim chance we can save them, I have to do it—I have to meet up with Dan.

"If you're going to meet him, take Ash," my wolf demands. But even if I wanted to, he'd kill him at first sight. He told him to get out of his territory, and if he's still there, then he's within his rights to murder him.

Me: What do you have that can help Benji?

I can almost feel the weight of his devious smile.

Dan: I have a vial that will help him. All the doctor needs to do is give it to him through the IV. But...

I wait for him to say what he needs to say next, and I know it won't be good.

Dan: It will come at a price.

Fuck! Of course, it does. I knew it wasn't going to be easy but still a part of me had hoped.

Me: Fine. Tell me where to meet you.

Dan: I'll drop you a pin.

Me: This better not be a trap.

Dan: It's not.

Kat: How do I know for sure?

Dan: You don't. You'll just have to debate whether Benji's life is worth the risk.

I yank my hair in frustration. Fuck this guy! I can't believe I let him into my family's life for so long.

Dan: Oh, and Kat one more thing.

I wait impatiently, already tired of his games.

Dan: Come alone or you won't get the vial.

I guess that was easy since I wasn't planning on taking anyone else.

I grab the waist strap Amara gave me and put it in the backpack.

"Hey, Mom." I startle and turn back around. My kids are standing at the entrance to my room. One look at me and their faces fall. "What happened?" I can taste Ava's fear and as if that wasn't enough, both of their hearts are racing.

"It looks like Benji and Tyler aren't doing so well," I let out a long breath. It's been a long day and the day isn't over, at least not for me.

"I thought they were getting better?" Ezra stares down at his hands. We've only known them for a week, but already they've managed to create bonds with my kids that their own father never could, and it's obvious that I'm not the only one emotionally invested.

“We thought so too but he took a turn for the worse. Tyler is trying to help him out but it’s draining too much of his life.” My vision blurs but I hold in my tears wanting to be strong, not only for them, but myself too.

“And where are you going?” Ava narrows her eyes and crosses her arms. She looks like a miniature version of myself.

“Don’t you have to work?”

“Mom,” she gives me a strange look. “I just got off.” Shit, it’s later than I thought.

I sigh. “I might have a chance to help Benji and Tyler, so I’m going to take it. You two better go to sleep early.” I mostly say this because I don’t want Az and Ash trying to pry information out of them. I walk past them, kissing them both on the cheek, and take off looking at my phone to figure out what route to take.

When I get outside, I quietly take off my clothes and throw them off to the side. There’s no point in ruining an expensive outfit the guys bought me. I shift into a wolf, clutch my backpack between my teeth, and run off into the woods. When I come across the wards that keep me inside the property, I hesitate. I look around to see if anyone has spotted me, but it’s a dark night with no shifters in sight. I make my way across the barrier and nothing stops me. There’s no wall in place. I give a triumphant howl then remember I have to stay quiet. I’m the only one who can't cross the wards, but all the others can.

Amara forgot to put the wards up or she probably got too busy. Either way, it works out for me. I don't know how I would've been able to convince the guys to let me go otherwise. Ash would have immediately said no if I had mentioned Dan's name, and Az would have looked at me with those pretty blue eyes and left me hanging, which would have been a clear no from him.

I set my pace, hopeful that this isn't a trap and that he'll give me what he has to cure Benji. But that's in a perfect world and I have never lived in one.

It's been hours of running. The only reason I'm not scared to go out this late is because I have perfect night vision, and I'll be able to track my steps back home, and if any supernaturals try to attack, I know my dagger will give me a fighting chance.

I hope I'm long gone by the time the guys find out I've left. I'm sure they'll be furious once they realize I'm not home, but once they find out I did it for Tyler and Benji, I'm sure all will be forgiven. At least, I hope.

I think I'm the only predator out here. If not, I have that handy blade in my backpack that I can use to cut a bitch. I also packed some clothes to get dressed right before I get to my destination. The last thing I want to do is show up in front of Dan naked.

I stop running and look up. There's rustling that is out of place in the forest. My hair stands to attention as I look over my shoulder, realizing too late that someone is watching me.

Chapter Fourteen

Ash

I still don't completely trust Katarina. This is the reason I have her messages going to my phone.

"That's an invasion of privacy." My wolf is pissed. He actually likes Katarina and her wolf.

"Oh, don't start with me," I say, cutting that shit out before it goes any further.

I told Az about who she's meeting, and he wanted to come too, but someone needed to be there for our brothers. He'd probably try killing Dante before he figured out if there was something to help Benji and Tyler. I know Katarina would be hesitant to ask me because she'd be afraid that I'd kill him on the spot, and normally I would have, but I have to see if what he's saying is true.

He finally agreed to stay behind, but it took a lot of convincing. He and I are a lot alike. We're both determined and hate being the one to stay back when things are out of our control. We all hate it, but it never takes too much to convince Benji and Tyler. Tyler can't argue as much since he's an expert at doing the computer shit none of us want to do, and usually, Benji handles all the wiring of bombs, so most of the time, Az and I are at the forefront of conflicts.

Katarina knows someone is trailing her and she picks up her pace. Didn't I tell her people are after her? She's going to put both of us in danger. But there's a small spark of hope, and because of that, I'm taking my chances. Amara didn't get to put up the wards, Katarina got lucky and was able to leave without having to ask anyone to let her out.

She suddenly stops looking around. She can feel my presence but not enough to smell who it is yet. It'll be a hell of a surprise when she finds out it's me. She tried being really quiet about it, thinking she was being discreet, but I've been watching her since she left the hospital. I saw her run through the forest, pumping her legs trying to reach our house as fast as she could, and I watched as she came back out with a backpack. She shifted and ran with the pack in her mouth.

I immediately knew something was wrong when she didn't put up a fight with Doc to let her stay the night with them. They're the only ones she's been able to keep a relationship with, so naturally she'd want to be there for everything that goes down. That's why I didn't ask her to come early in the morning. I thought she would never leave their sides, and the doctors needed to keep them stable.

I make sure to keep a good distance and travel downwind so that she won't be able to smell me. I watch her put her backpack down and shift into a human. She opens her bag and pulls out clothes, underwear, a bra, jeans, socks, sneakers, a band tee that looks oddly like Benji's, and a hoodie that I think belongs to Tyler. He always wears that thing everywhere.

My eyes trail down, trying to linger over her body, but I make myself turn away to give her privacy, only turning back around when I hear the zipper on her pack close.

"Maybe you should give her something more useful than a tie. Then she would be wearing something of ours." My wolf sounds a little jealous she didn't bring something that smells like us.

"No," I snap at him. I don't want her to have something else that belongs to us. I don't know why I left the tie there in the first place. I shouldn't have entertained the idea. It's like a betrayal to *her* that I gave Katarina something that belongs to me.

"You're being stubborn," he chastises me. *"You know what this means. She's trying to wear your clothing."* He emphasizes every word.

"Don't... Don't start with that shit," I grumble. "Our opportunity for a mate died out a long time ago." I try to stop the carousel of images in my head from that painful day and focus on the woman ahead of me instead.

She looks at her phone frequently, no doubt making sure she's heading in the right direction. She still hasn't learned how to walk quietly. Her feet are so loud they're alerting all the predators who are near and far. It'll take her years of practice before she can learn how to be silent. Her wolf is at least graceful. We walk for more than forty-five minutes when she suddenly stops, her posture is tense and she looks wildly around, waiting for something, or specifically someone.

My body stiffens letting go of a growl. I can smell him before I see him. What the fuck is he doing here? I didn't think he was stupid enough to do it himself. Memories of telling him to get the fuck out of my territory crash down. I should make an example out of him. It's not like the council isn't already tracking him. He's going to put Katarina in more danger.

I shift into a human, not caring if I'm completely naked, finally making my presence known and standing next to her. Katarina's eyes widen and her posture changes, realizing it was me tracking her. "I told him to stop texting me," she says as a way to defend herself, making her look even more guilty in my eyes. I fold my arms across my chest trying to look more intimidating, but not for her, for him.

Before I can stop myself, I growl out, "Why are you here Katarina, and why didn't you tell me?" I can't come out and tell her I'd been snooping. Tyler will no doubt figure it out and throw a fit my way. He's so in love with her, he won't notice if she ever decides to betray us. I had to get Matt, a beta of the pack, to help me link her new phone to mine.

She looks up at me with a slight hint of annoyance, the surprised look gone. "You're really trying to act like my daddy? I don't have to tell you anything about my life." Sarcasm drips from her tongue. The way she says daddy sends a shivering heat low in my belly that flickers...something akin to hope—ahhh no, that can't be right, she's messing with my body and my mind.

She's right of course, but it doesn't stop me from feeling a pang of something I don't want to decipher right now.

"I told you to come alone, Kat." Dante doesn't pay me any attention, which stirs my wolf. I need to keep my shit contained before I snap his neck. Katarina had the right idea of not wanting to bring me. She was afraid I'd kill him before he was able to talk, and it's starting to look like she's probably right. The only thing I'm thinking about is the vial he told her about. After he gives it to us, I'm not letting him leave. I'll finish him once and for all.

"He followed me." She looks at him with pleading eyes, and I fucking hate that she gives him any look besides anger and disgust. "I didn't know he followed me until about two seconds ago." She looks at me, narrowing her eyes. She's probably pissed that I didn't make myself known, but I was loud as hell to give her a chance to figure it out. It's on her that she dismissed her senses so quickly.

He stands way too close to Katarina, and a deep rumble comes out of my throat. It's low and threatening and there's no doubt of my intention of wanting him to take ten steps back.

"Calm down, wolf, remember she isn't ours." My wolf and I are always on the same page, except for this. He thinks she belongs to us but she doesn't. I know that for a fact. I met the person who truly belonged to me and my brothers a long time ago, but I lost her.

"I don't have much time." Her voice quivers slightly. "Dan, give me what I came here for."

"I've been trying to contact you, but you don't respond," he says, ignoring me as he gazes at her longingly and my body gets twitchy. If he proves to be useless, I'll take his worthless life now.

I don't care if his pack comes after us. We're more ruthless than any other pack in existence. We were trained in a special unit to serve the council a lifetime ago. I shiver at the memory of what they made us do; we hated it. But they needed the skills we had, and they took whatever they wanted without consequences.

"You shouldn't be trying to get a hold of her," I snarl. "I should just kill you right here and now." It's like my wolf takes over. I'm usually the calm before the storm, but I can't wait. My wolf sees him as a threat to Katarina and wants to take him out.

After the shit he's put her through, he's still trying to make himself look like the good guy.

"I have important information," he says smugly. As if that will keep me from ripping his neck open. "I know someone that can help you. That can help us escape." My wolf seethes and I want to start pacing back and forth. If Az were here, this guy would already be dead.

I open my mouth to tell him to fuck off, but he continues. "I know, Kat, that I haven't been forthcoming, but I didn't want to scare you." His voice is gentle and he looks sympathetic. I'm sure he's used that tone with a lot of women to get exactly what he wants.

I'm not convinced. Fuck this, I can't listen to his dumb shit anymore. Moving fast as lightning, I wrap my hand around his neck, and his eyes widen in surprise, not expecting me to move and try to kill him. "It's about Benji," he chokes out, finally answering his first statement. I loosen my hand but only slightly to let him talk.

"Spit it out." I grit my teeth. "My patience is running thin." My eyes change color, assessing the man under my grip.

I want blood.

I can almost taste the warm liquid that will run down my arm if I puncture his neck just a tiny bit harder.

Katarina gasps. I briefly move my gaze to hers. I don't think she's ever seen me lose control, and I hope she never has to see that side of me.

Dante coughs and I loosen up slightly in case he really has important information that can save my brothers. I don't want to ruin the slim chance if we ever had one.

"What information do you have that's so important you had me meet you in the middle of nowhere?" She extends her hand out to the forest, pointing out the obvious.

I laugh. "You actually think he has information. All he wants to do is get close to you." Yeah, I know what I said, but I have to make sure no one knows of the tiny sliver of hope that I'm currently holding on to.

"She belongs to me, Ash," he says, his tone full of anger. "But I do come with information, and it has to do with Kat. I also have the vial for Benji."

His voice is hoarse and desperate because I start squeezing harder again.

Katarina gets even closer to him, and my wolf shouts a warning. *"Protect her."* But I still have Dante by the neck, and it feels too good to stop. I'd love to take the life of a man that's become a thorn in my side.

"I was able to get Kat out of your wards because of a witch," he pleads, and I pause for a second, still gripping him tightly. I've wondered how the hell he was able to get past them. No one should have been able to. He tries to cough. "We made a deal. She was going to help me get Kat out and I helped her slip something to Benji. I'm here to warn Kat and take her with me. I have to protect her," he wheezes, my wolf hating the way he thinks he can come here and take her from us.

"She's not going anywhere with you." My voice booms through the stillness of the forest and even Katarina flinches.

"Please Kat, I can protect you." He tries to look at her but I tighten my grip on his neck so he can't. All he can do is see what I let him see. Who's he trying to protect her from? The council? Why is he so worried about protecting her? He's the one that put a target on her back.

She looks to be in deep thought for a moment. "Are you actually thinking about his offer?" I breathe heavier and clench my jaw in annoyance.

"Where were *you* when she needed protecting?" I dig my nails into his skin and shake him against my chest. He narrows his eyes as he turns purple. "She was attacked yesterday. I at least sent her out with a witch. But you, you didn't do shit." He was obviously tracking her. Why didn't he help her out when she was ambushed?

"I wasn't tracking her phone," he falters.

"Sure you weren't," I say disapprovingly, looking over at Katarina.

She looks at me and my heart drops, I want to know what she's thinking. She's hard to read because she's facing away from me. "You think that you can protect me?" She laughs bitterly while he holds on to hope. "You didn't do anything while Theo treated me like shit. How do I know you're not just going to stand around and do nothing," she screams out in frustration.

"I won't." He pissed me off again so I'm squeezing his neck just a little tighter, preventing air from going into his lungs.

"The witch will protect me, and I'll protect her." He's dumber than he looks if he actually thinks that someone will actually protect him.

A thought occurs to me. "Did she make you turn Katarina?" Her head turns to the side while her eyes turn violet.

"She told me that once she turned, I could have her and she'd protect us." Fucking idiot. This

dumbass wanted some witch to protect them-
, there's no way he can keep Katarina safe in the supernatural world.

He opens his mouth to say more when an arrow goes straight through his chest, and I drop him to the ground in surprise. Katarina lets out a high-pitched scream and pulls out a glowing dagger from thin air. What the fuck is that? Is that the Kiss of Death Amara told us about?

She stops screaming, bends down with shaky fingers, and searches through Dante's pockets. I don't think she'll find what she's looking for. I knew it was impossible. Dante didn't have anything we needed. He was lying, all he wanted was for Katarina to go with him. But that small, very tiny sliver of hope is why I entertained the idea.

I look at Dante's body with a low growl, wishing I had been the one to end his miserable life. After scanning the silent tree line, I bend and rip the arrow from Dante, looking it over in disbelief. It's been years since I've seen a custom arrow like this one, with a red cedar shaft and the distinct broadhead made of silver. The arrow of a hunter. "We have to go, now!" Katarina gives me a triumphant look as she stands, but it vanishes quickly as she remembers the threat at hand. She scans the forest with the glint of a predator in her eyes, and I know her wolf is peaking up, determined to chase them down.

I can't let that happen.

I sniff the air and catch a whiff of the unfamiliar scent closing in on us. But this can't be right, the hunters have been gone for many years.

I lunge for her arm before she does something stupid, but she moves quickly, and I only grasp air. "Those are hunters," I hiss, trying to get her to safety. "Katarina," I plead desperately. "We have to go." Her violet eyes glow, making her look less like a human.

"Why?" she snaps. "If we don't go after them, they'll kill us both, and I'm not ready to die." She tilts her head to the side assessing me. "Did you send them after Dan and me?" Katarina asks, shaking from anger instead of fear.

"Do I strike you as the kind of man to hand off my dirty work to someone else, Katarina?" I cluck my tongue disapprovingly. There's a look of understanding slowly inching across her angry features, and I finally grab her wrist and pull her body into my chest. "If I wanted you dead, Katarina, I'd have slipped into the hot tub with you earlier and wrapped my hands around that pretty little neck until it fucking snapped in two." Her eyes widen, but we don't have time for her to be pissy about her lack of privacy. "Now fucking MOVE," I snap, dragging her to the woods until we're sprinting through the thick trees.

Our legs pump through the tall grass, and I can see Kat slowing down. She's not used to running this much. She's years of training behind where she needs to be to keep up with us, but she keeps pushing through.

I want to tell her to shift into a wolf so that she can use it to help maintain speed, but the hunters are hot on our trail. There is no way for her to transition safely.

There's only one thing left to do. I stop immediately. She was sent to me to protect, and that's exactly what I'm going to do.

"What are you doing?" she shouts, panting hard. She glances back, her eyes wildly watching for the hunters that aren't far behind. "They're going to catch up to us. Come on." She tries to grab my hand and I pull her away. She looks at me with desperation in her eyes. Her human side is back, but I need her wolf, her wolf is more fearless and doesn't second guess her steps. I briefly remember the first encounter I had when she tried to attack me. That is what we need right now.

"Go." I motion with my head. "Once you no longer hear footsteps, shift into your wolf. Use your senses, they will take you back to safety." She opens her mouth to talk but I put my hand up to stop her. "Trust your instincts. Has your wolf ever let you down?" She looks down to hide how scared she is and shakes her head. "I'll be fine," I reassure her.

She looks back at me slowly, and I don't miss the way she trails my body with her lingering gaze or the way she bites her lip, as if there's something more she needs to say. I stand a little straighter as she shakes her head definitely.

"I can't leave you," she says sadly. It's as if something is holding her back. "Please, just come with me. We'll try to outrun them." She swallows hard, and I suspect she's trying to hold in a sob.

"Kat, go now." My Alpha tone is strident, the command vibrating through her regardless of her need to disobey. Her legs begin to move, forced to follow me like the rest of the pack. After one last look at her retreating back, I shift into a wolf.

It's been a long time since we've had to deal with hunters, and truthfully, we all thought they died out.

There are about seven surrounding me. My wolf and I are in sync, turning in a circle to assess the biggest threat. I jump after him, sinking my canines right through his throat in one swift movement.

Blood drips from my clenched jaw as the sting of an arrow hits my thigh. A growl rips from my throat, but I don't have time to react before it's raining arrows. Dozens of them fly in a perfect arc through the air. One sinks into each of my calves, and two plunge deep into my sides. I count six of those silver-tipped bastards before I go down hard.

Chapter Fifteen

Az

I don't have a good feeling about this. I keep adjusting my red cufflinks.

I should have gone with my gut and followed them. Something about this doesn't sit right, but we were too desperate to get my brothers better, it was like grasping at straws.

Benji is not looking any better, so we had to take the chance. I stare at my uneaten plate of food on the table. I get up, and instead of going to see if anything has changed with my brothers, I push the door open, the need to hunt coursing through me. I hate this so much, it's not like me to stand on the sidelines feeling useless. I need to hunt and kill. The need overwhelms my senses to think as anything but a beast.

When I look over the tree line, I see a black wolf running my way. I hesitate for a brief moment before recognizing Kat holding a backpack in her mouth. I'd laugh at how goofy she looks but quickly notice she's not with my brother.

Something has happened. A low, wary growl emanates from my mouth, and I rush to meet her in the middle.

Her bones start to readjust and her body switches back to human. "What happened?" I look into her eyes, waiting for an explanation. My heart is thundering in my chest so close to exploding into pieces. I'm usually composed, but when it comes to my brothers, I worry about each of them.

"Hunters." Her eyes are wild, which doesn't help calm my nerves.

"Hunters?" I repeat back, no that's not possible, she's mistaken. She hasn't been a part of our world for long, she has it wrong. They have not existed for a long time.

"I'm not crazy, Az," she pants as if she knows where my thoughts are heading. That's a disturbing feeling. I hate being exposed to her. She comes closer to me, and I try to keep my eyes from wandering down her naked body. "You need to go, he needs your help." Her voice is urgent, bringing me back to the problem at hand.

She unzips her backpack and I clench my jaw trying not to show how much it bothers me that it smells of Benji and Tyler. She hands me a vial and I take it from her hands, careful not to touch her skin because when I do, it ignites a fire I don't want to think about.

"This is supposed to help Benji," she says, her eyes softening a bit before the fear returns. My eyes widen in surprise that they actually got it. I thought for sure it was a trap for him to kidnap her and that Ash and Kat would come back with nothing. This shit better work or I'm hunting Dante down.

"Where is he?" I ask, worried nerves clawing up my stomach.

"I can take you there." Her body sags as if she's remembering the long trip, but she'd endure it anyway to save Ash. Even if he's been nothing but an asshole to her.

Before she can say anything else, I stop her. "No." She looks like she's going to argue, "I can smell your tracks." She looks behind her and back up at me, nodding with understanding. I start unbuttoning my red shirt. "You can go back to the hospital to see Benji, he needs it." I hand it back to her. She looks like she wants to say something else but stops herself.

I watch her shift before taking the antidote in her mouth and running away. I take off the rest of my clothes and immediately shift.

My wolf instincts take over, finding Kat's tracks and running through the forest. Her scent is everywhere, and my wolf would roll around in it if we weren't so desperate to find my brother.

After running for a while, I spot a place where she hung out for a couple minutes longer. I stop and take my time to sniff. This hopefully means I'm close. I start tracking again when I smell blood.

There's a pool of blood on the ground, but I already know it's not my brother's. It smells like Dante. Good, he finally got the ending he deserves. I just hope I'm not too late for my brother. I catch another whiff of Ash's scent and follow it to a cabin out in the middle of fucking nowhere.

I walk around the area before getting close. I don't want these fuckers to take me by surprise. I bide my time, anxious to get to Ash, but I know that timing is everything. Even if I have to wait until the next day, so be it. I just hope my brother will make it another day.

Three men get into the truck, and I wait a while before pacing around again. There are more in there, I can smell them.

I walk closer to the cabin hearing voices. This is one of my favorite parts of hunting. When the prey doesn't know the big bad wolf is hiding in the shadows, ready to attack.

I look through the third small window and find Ash tied to a chair. They're talking to him, but I'm not tuning into their conversation. My main focus is on figuring out how to kill them and get Ash out of there safely.

I go back to the front and turn into a human again, surprised when I try the knob and it opens. These guys probably think no one will come out, but you can never be too careful.

I hear them talking toward the back of the house. My footsteps are soft. The floorboards are creaking softly, but not enough to startle them. I grab the crossbow from the table, checking to see if it's loaded correctly, and adjusting the sight before moving on.

My brother has already sensed me. He starts laughing while the other men try to figure out what's going on with him. His eyes are wild, and blood pools from his mouth onto his chest. He looks like a psycho.

I take that moment to make an appearance, lifting the crossbow up and immediately hitting one of the men in the chest. He goes down quickly. One of the other men tries to attack me when he realizes what's going on, but I put another arrow in the crossbow.

Instead of shooting him, I swing the crossbow wide, connecting with his face and spraying blood all over the brown wall. The other guy manages to shoot me on my side, catching me by surprise.

"Fuck, that hurts," I say as I pry it from my side. Using the same arrow that I was shot with, I slam it right into the guy's skull while he's struggling to load his bow. The man goes down.

I quickly untie Ash from the ropes, but my hand stands still when he says, "They're not after wolves, they're after Katarina."

Chapter Sixteen

Ash

"Why?" Az asks, scrunching his eyebrows together. He's the only person I know that can untie ropes that quickly.

"They didn't want to kill me from what they were saying, they just wanted info on her," I tell him as he yanks the arrows from my legs. We don't heal as quickly from the wounds inflicted by silver, and the bastards left the arrows in my legs to weaken me.

"Are they even hunters?" he asks. I shrug, they smell just like hunters. "Did they say what they wanted with Kat?"

"No. They wouldn't say."

"How is Katarina doing?" I know she made it home since Az is here, but I want to reassure myself that she got back safely. It's not because I care about her, it's because she has the vial that can help my brothers.

"Sure, keep telling yourself that." My wolf narrows his eyes.

"She made it and brought the antidote with her." My brows shoot up in surprise. I breathe a sigh of relief at finally being able to confirm she made it home safely with the cure. "I guess Dante wasn't lying." I just hope it's not poison that will kill him faster. Because if it's something that will harm him, I'll bring Dante back from the dead and kill him again.

I try to stand up, but my legs are in pain, so I sit right back down. "I need a few more minutes to get rid of the numbness before I can shift."

"Don't worry, if anyone comes, I can take them down." Az looks down at the crossbow, but he doesn't need it. He usually uses his hands or mouth to dismember someone. "So what happened when you guys met Dante?" he growls when he says his name and I chuckle. The feeling is mutual.

"Well, he of course wanted to take Katarina back," I say with a slight hint of anger, and it bothers me that I care more than I should. She means nothing to me, I remind myself. The only reason I'm tolerating her presence is because Amara asked us to protect her.

"Did you kill him?" Az asks, looking hopeful that he died a horrible death.

"No, but an arrow went through him. I think he's dead." Az doesn't look convinced.

"I could smell his blood but there was no body, Ash," he narrows his gaze in thought.

"I saw him go down man, he looked pretty fucking dead. I'm sure an animal already got to his body by now."

"Are there any more hunters?" Az asks, looking out the window as if waiting for another attack. We can never be too careful. Working for the council has taught us that.

"From what I know, it was just the three," I tell him, trying to get feeling back into my legs.

Az is looking out the window contemplating whether to ask me something. "Just spit it out," I tell him, my patience running thin. Being hurt will do that to you.

"You really don't think Kat is meant for us?" He purposely avoids eye contact with me because he knows that question makes him look like he might care slightly for her.

"No," I say, cutting that shit out before he goes any further. "I met our mate once, and she was the one I felt pulled to."

"Yeah." He scratches the back of his head. "But... You said there was no spark."

“That still doesn’t mean that the goddess didn’t make her ours.” There is a small spark of hope before it vanishes.

My ears immediately zone in on low voices outside. My brother turns around to face me. “We have to go.”

“I still can’t feel my legs, Az. I can’t move.” I look around the room to see if anything can prop me up. I hate feeling like dead weight.

“Shit,” he says, before he picks me up from the chair and carries me. He walks as fast as he can out the door and into the protection of the forest. We probably look silly, two grown ass men, butt naked, one carrying the other with our dicks flopping around. We don’t care though, this is survival.

He puts me down and we wait silently for the men to arrive. The truck pulls up and my body tenses slightly, but not from fear. I’ve been in so many situations like this, I’ve lost count. It’s more of them trying to find Katarina.

“You have to kill them,” Az only nods his head, not paying me any attention. His focus is on the scene ahead of him.

Once they’re inside he approaches the cabin. He’s like a ghost the way he walks through the woods, but we were trained killers, courtesy of the council.

There’s commotion inside, which means they’ve already found the dead bodies. He slips back into the cabin in silence, and the next moment I hear screaming and gunshots. Az emerges a moment later with blood on his body and a stern resolve.

"They're dead," he tells me like it's not a big deal, and to us, it's not, this is just another day. "How are your legs?"

I test them out and the feeling has returned. That silver to wolves is no joke. We're hard to kill, but if the silver hits the wrong spot, we're dead. "Good," I say before turning into a wolf.

We make it a few steps before we catch her scent.

The witch's scent.

The scent we've spent a lifetime tracking.

She's here, which means Dante was working with her.

Chapter Seventeen

Kat

It's almost midnight by the time I make it to the doctor's office. I turn into a human, not caring that I'm fully naked. Now I understand why this is normal for shifters. You can't really be bothered to care when you have to do this constantly. I'm not going to lie; it was really hard for me to keep my eyes on Az when all I wanted to do was drag my eyes down to where his hands were unbuttoning his red shirt.

"Not now. We can think about what his sexy body looks like later, but right now we've got to get this to Benji," my wolf says with worry.

She's right. I put my lust-filled mind behind me and focus. "Hey Kat," the nurse says from the front desk. "Did you bring something to help him?" Well shit, I guess by now everyone knows what I went to do. The nurse looks hopeful, and I'm scared about what's waiting for me.

I walk into one of the rooms, and if it weren't for the nurse propping me up, I'd have fallen to the floor. My heart rate picks up, and a bead of sweat trails down my back.

Benji looks deathly pale, worse than before. I didn't know it was possible to look this bad and still be alive.

"Here, you can wear this." She gives me a nightgown, and I absentmindedly take it from her hands and put it on.

"Thank you," I say, trying to manage a smile, but I'm too tired for niceties.

"I'll get the doc so that he can give it to him," she says as she inspects the vial. Her face is full of skepticism there, and I'm so scared that this will kill him faster.

I'm itching to crawl into his side and hold him, but I'm too scared to see how terrible he looks up close.

I hesitantly walk forward as the nurse holds my hand in support. There's a purple tint to the dark circles under his eyes, and his lips are chapped and cracked. His breathing has slowed down drastically.

I lower my head and kiss his forehead gently. He doesn't stir, which has me worried. It was worth it though, meeting Dan and encountering the hunters. I hope that Ash made it out safely. I don't doubt his capabilities. He's one tough Alpha and adding Az to the mix...yeah. Those hunters don't stand a chance.

"Hey, love," I whisper as if not wanting to spook him. The sound of the heart monitor is slowing down. "I brought you medication that will make you better." I don't add that I *hope* it makes him better. It's a big probability he won't make it. He doesn't stir and that scares me. "Oh, and get this, hunters still exist. I didn't want to leave Ash, but I had to if I wanted to bring you the medicine. I told Az and he left a little while ago to look for Ash," I tell him, wondering if he's able to hear me. "You better stay alive," I say, playing with the ends of my hair to keep my hands busy. "I'm going to be pissed if you're not trying. There's something I need to tell you when you're awake and that is—" I get close to his ear to whisper, "I'm in love with you," I murmur, pulling back when I hear footsteps getting closer.

Amara and Dr. Jones come in, both looking rundown. "I checked it and I can't sense any harmful spells." She gives it to the doc, and he goes to one of the tables off to the side. I watch as he uses a syringe to insert the needle, pulling out the plunger and emptying the fluid inside the glass bottle.

He comes back to where Benji is laying down and unscrews a cap that's connected to a tube. Amara hands him a piece of cloth that smells like alcohol. Doc uses it to clean it and hands it back to her. He inserts the syringe, twisting it before he uses his thumb to push back on the plunger, emptying the liquid and pulling it back out.

I hold my breath. Is it going to work? Did Dan give me something poisonous to kill him?

I walk over to Tyler's side. He looks exhausted from giving Benji some of his energy. I look at his heart rate on the monitor, and it appears to be stable, but his face looks drained. This antidote better work.

I'm on pins and needles waiting to see what will happen. I miss Benji's laid-back exterior. He acts like nothing bugs him, but in reality, he cares too deeply. I never thought I'd miss the nickname he'd given me, but after not hearing it for a couple of days, all I want is for him to call me Kitty Kat every day for the rest of my life.

I miss Tyler's beautiful dimples. The way he nerds out about computers. How easy going he is and how effortless it is to talk to him. I don't know what I would do without him.

"It'll be a while before the medication takes effect." Doc looks at me with kind eyes. It's hard to imagine this man as a doctor by how young he looks. I suppose it's the same with the lawyer. "Get some clothes on, maybe grab a shower and get some sleep, then come back here. He should be waking up by the time you get back in the morning." All I can do is hope the medication works. If not, I'm finding Dan's body and looking for a necromancer. I'm sure something like that exists and having them bring him to life just so I can kill him again sounds satisfying.

"I don't want to leave," I say quietly.

"There is nothing more we can do today. The medication should hopefully start working soon. I'll be keeping an eye on him through the night," Amara says gently. "I'll have the guys call you if anything happens." I look at her warily, but I'd probably be driving the staff nuts.

Not wanting to leave but knowing I need the sleep, I say, "Thanks, Doc." He nods as I get up from the chair and walks out after me.

"I have to check on other patients, but I'll be here when you get back," he assures me with one of his winning smiles.

When he walks away, I hand the nurse the robe she gave me. "Thanks," I tell her before walking out into the brisk air. It's way past the kids' bedtime, so I hope they're already asleep.

I shift into a wolf, loving the fresh air. There is something about being out at night by yourself. Sometimes you just need to be with your thoughts. It's been a long week, from getting bit and turning into a wolf to developing feelings, moving from my home, finally getting a job, divorcing my husband, being kidnapped and now possibly losing the two men I've developed feelings for.

The tension releases slightly but not much since Ash and Az haven't gotten home. As much as I hate those two assholes, I hope they do make it back safely.

I grab some clothes from the backpack and put on my shorts and a shirt and walk into the house. I can hear my kids in the kitchen eating loudly. "Mom!" Ezra shouts. "We were so worried." His knees are bouncing up and down but immediately come to a stop when he sees me.

I smile sadly. "Sorry, there was a small chance that I could help Tyler and Benji and I wanted to take it."

"Are they going to get better?" Ava holds her breath, her cheeks turning slightly pink.

"I sure hope so," I say, staring at their sugary cereal and wanting to tell them they shouldn't eat that before bed, but I'm too tired to have this conversation.

Ava lets out her breath slowly. "You eat up and go to bed. You have school tomorrow." Actually, more like in a few hours.

Instead of groans, they look excited. This school must be run differently than their regular school, but as long as they're learning what they're supposed to, I'm happy to keep them here.
"Love you both. Goodnight." They mumble their goodnights as they munch on cereal. My feet feel

like heavy rocks as I climb the stairs. Each step is harder to take than the last.

I wash up, brush my teeth, and get ready for bed.

It's been hours tossing and turning before I'm able to sleep, and just when I'm drifting off, there's a knock on my door. I almost groan but then remember it might be news on Tyler and Benji, so I quickly get up from bed and answer it.

Az and Ash's large bodies fill every inch of my doorway. They both look exhausted, covered in a slick sheen of sweat and blood. They have robes draped over their bodies as I survey them for injuries. It would have been shitty if I saved two of the guys by getting their brothers killed. I'm glad they made it back alive.

"We need to talk," Ash says as he waltzes into my room with Az on his heels.

"Sure, just come on in," I say, more to myself than them since they're already inside. I close the door and sit on the bed while they look slightly uncomfortable looking for a place to sit. They settle for standing, staring directly in front of me.

I stifle a yawn when Az starts speaking in that low, husky tone of his. "Where's the dagger?" I sit up straighter, not because I'm surprised that they mentioned it, but because I know Amara probably told them about it. I actually thought they'd come to me sooner. Ash is probably already speculating that I've killed numerous humans, did dark magic, and was gifted with it by demons.

But the real reason I'm slightly freaking out is because it's hidden in my treasure drawer... The drawer I use to stuff their belongings in.

"Oh umm..." I tug on my hair trying to figure out a way out of this mess. "I'll show you guys, but you have to turn around."

They look at me like I've lost my mind, then at each other as they silently communicate. Ash finally sighs and they both turn around.

I walk to my drawer next to my bed, the whole time my eyes are on them making sure they're not peeking. I open it gently, moving items from the guys and grabbing my weapon. I place the clothing, pillowcase, and the tie back in and close it. As soon as I do, they turn around, their eyes taking in what I'm holding.

Az comes closer to me, mesmerized by it. "How did you get this?" He keeps his eyes on it.

"The second night I worked at the Crescent Lounge two ladies came up to me—"

"What did they look like?" Ash crosses his arms, narrowing his eyes on me like maybe he thinks I've had it for a while and have been hiding it this whole time.

"Well, they're twins, I think. One had dark skin and the other had light skin, both with beautiful long hair. They looked young, but the way they spoke to me said otherwise. They went by the names of Imani and Althea." They give each other a look I can't quite decipher, so I continue. "They said they were keeping it for me." I want to tell them to go ask Benji, but he can't even open his eyes, much less talk, so I'm on my own.

"Let me see it," Az asks, holding up his palm. I place it on his hand and he inspects it. "It's legit, Ash. She can use it to kill any supernatural with one swipe." They both shudder and I hope they're thinking twice about messing with me.

"Keep that away from us," Ash says with finality. Az hands it back to me. "Get some sleep Katarina, it's been a long night."

As soon as they leave, I place my dagger back inside the drawer and slip right to sleep, exhaustion overriding my body.

It feels like I haven't slept much when I get a call. I grab it immediately, but I don't recognize the number.

"Hey, Kat, it's Doc." My grogginess washes away and my heart pounds so fast that I'm surprised it hasn't made a dent in my chest. "You need to come down here now." Urgency laces every single word.

Chapter Eighteen

Kat

I hang up the phone, going through the drawers and picking up a shirt and some sweats. I scoop up my belt and tie it around my waist, grabbing the dagger and taking it with me. After everything that's happened, I don't feel safe without my blade.

I leave the house. It's early in the morning but still dark out. The chilly weather doesn't bother me as much as it did when I was human.

I was too scared to ask if they're dead. I don't know what I'll do if they are. My body trembles, feeling worried about what I'm going to find.

I run to the hospital by tracking my scent from last night. The adrenaline helps push my body harder than I ever have before. I open the doors and walk straight to their room, worried about what I'm going to find out.

I brace myself before I open the door. Please let them be okay. I chant over and over again in my head. My wolf has nothing to say, but she's moping around in a corner, head down, eyes closed.

I hold the tears that threaten to pour and open the door, making eye contact with Dr. Carter on my way in. "How are they, Doc?" Doctor Carter's face morphs into something I wasn't expecting from the urgency on the phone.

"Come see for yourself," Benji rasps. Oh shit! It actually worked!

My legs start walking before my mind can comprehend what I'm doing. My eyes widen when I see how much healthier he looks. He's not as pale as he was last night. So, if he's better, Tyler should be better too. Benji sees where my eyes are wandering and says, "He gave me a lot of his energy, he's still sleeping." I nod my head, tears of joy streaming down my face.

"How do you feel?" I croak out. I'm too vulnerable, but with him, it doesn't matter. I want him to see how worried I was for him. I want him to see the love I have for him even when I haven't told him yet.

"I've been better," he chokes out like he's feeling too emotional. "But having you here is worth it." He means because of what he went through with Dan.

I'm going to break out in a full sob, I can feel it. "Where are my brothers?" I panic slightly. I just saw them early this morning, have they not been here yet?

"Here we are," Ash says, always making a grand entrance.

"So, you guys encountered hunters?" As soon as the question leaves his mouth, I realize that he had to have heard the things I whispered to him while he was unconscious. He notices the look of utter shock on my face but continues. "I heard every single word. I was too exhausted to open my eyes or speak, but I could hear you." Well fuck!

Oh, well I guess I'm glad I didn't confess anything embarrassing. Oh no, wait, yes I did. I told him I loved him. I internally cringe. I probably should have waited, but I thought he was dying, and I was afraid he'd leave this world without knowing how much I love him.

"Yeah, we got them all," Az answers, and I whip my head around to face him. But he doesn't look at me at all. His eyes are assessing Benji, trying to get himself to realize that his brother is in fact doing better.

"Well, Az got them all. I couldn't walk," Ash breathes calmly as if he's letting go of all the tension he's had since—well, since I've arrived here.

"Yeah, it doesn't matter. You've saved my life more times than I can count," Az says, blowing Ash off.

"What does this mean?" Tyler asks, surprising me. My eyes flash and he smiles, showing me those dimples that I find so attractive. "Do we know why the hunters are back?" Benji looks at them attentively too.

Ash's eyes fall to me. "We'll discuss it all later." Really? Does he not trust me? I got the medication for Benji to help him, isn't that proof enough?

I want to snap at both of them but don't want to put any more stress on Benji and Tyler, so for now I'll bite my tongue. I thought Ash and I had made progress, but it doesn't look that way.

"Okay, everyone." The doc comes back in. "My patients need to get rest and you all need to get out." Low snarls come from Ash and Az. "Oh, no growling in my hospital, everyone out," he shouts, but not enough to be aggressive.

No one is fighting him, so I don't either. "Kat, wait," Benji says before I walk out the door.

I stop to turn. "Thank you for the antidote. "We..." he looks at Tyler then back at me, "would have died without it." As I sit on the edge of his bed, he grabs my face and I lean in close, our lips nearly touching, and give him a whisper of a kiss. He groans when I pull back. I hate it too, but I need him to heal.

"You both get better and then we can do other stuff." I wink at them both and they groan. "And you're welcome, Benji," I mutter, a grin taking over my face. I walk out the door but not before I say, "And maybe I'll finally get the chance to invite you into that shower you've been waiting for." Understanding crosses Benji's features, remembering the first day we met, and I wink with a promise before leaving.

Chapter Nineteen

Kat

I run back home by myself since the guys stayed behind to see other patients making sure they're okay. If they didn't hate me so much, I'd think they were decent leaders for always looking out for their people.

I make it to the house just in time. My kids haven't left for school. They're still eating at the kitchen bar. "Hey." They look more alert than usual this morning, especially for going to bed so late last night. "Morning, Lily." She has dark circles under her eyes that I'm sure mirror my own.

They smile warily, staring at me intently waiting for news. "The guys are doing much better." The energy in the room shifts and the relief is evident in the way their bodies sag.

Lily puts her hand on her chest. "That's really good news. I'll have to give Benji a piece of my mind, and Tyler too, for trying to be a savior and draining his energy. Those boys are going to give me a heart attack," she says as she turns back around to finish up breakfast. "I'm going to bring them something good to eat, none of that hospital garbage." She goes into the pantry, grabbing two Tupperware bowls with lids. "They need some of my food if they want to recover." I watch her as she closes it and grabs a bag from one of the drawers to put it in.

She hands me a plate with scrambled eggs and bacon, and when I sit down, I'm surprised I'm starving.

"Doc kicked us out," I warn. "He might tell you to leave."

She waves her hand. "I don't have to walk in and see them, I just want to make sure they're getting the right nutrition." She tosses a big bag over her rounded shoulder and walks out the door that leads outside.

It's now or never.

I bite my lip, trying to figure out the best way to tell my kids that I'm dating two men. Worry gnaws on me that they're not going to accept this new relationship dynamic or that they don't want me to see other people.

"Oh, this again." My wolf sounds irritated. *"Just come out and say it. You'll just get yourself more anxious holding this all in."*

"So..." They both snap their heads in my direction with dread in their eyes, sitting up straighter and waiting to see what I'm going to say next. "I'm dating Tyler and Benji."

"MOM!" Ava shouts. Scaring the shit out of me. "You really have got to stop doing that." She palms the sides of her face in frustration.

"Seriously," Ezra agrees, taking another bite of his food.

"What do you mean?" I'm dumbfounded by their annoyance.

"You made it sound like it's something bad, something serious," she groans.

"This is serious."

"Okay, it is, but not the way you think," Ezra chimes in, leaning back in his chair and crossing his arms.

"I'm not following." I look between them, waiting for an explanation.

Ava throws her arms in the air. "We don't care that you date them. You're probably going to end up dating Az and Ash too, and that's fine—" I open my mouth to tell them that's a hell no, but she puts a hand up to stop me. "The way you make it sound like it's a life-or-death situation when it's not. So what? You're dating two men and probably will date another two more. We just want you to be happy. It doesn't matter to us. But, for the love of God, stop being so dramatic when you talk that way. It freaks us out."

I guess they have a point. I've been known to get a little out of hand when I talk. According to Jess, I would scare her when I would bring certain conversations up. She says that I make them sound so dramatic. I blame the Spanish telenovelas I watched trying to teach myself how to speak Spanish.

"Agree with all of that." Ezra grabs his plate and Ava's and takes them to the sink.

My wolf is in the background narrowing her eyes and chuckling at the same time. Well, I think that went well.

I hear heavy footsteps before Ava puts her phone down on the table and jumps off the stool and goes to open the door that leads outside.

"I'll be right back," she tells me.

Cara, Tiffany, and Bryson walk in with Lily right behind them. "Hey!" Ava says to them. Her grin widens when she sees her friends.

"How are the guys doing?" Bryson asks, looking a little tired himself.

"Mom said that they're doing a lot better." He lets his head fall back in relief. Cara and Tiffany exhale like they were holding onto a breath.

"You three sit." Lily points to the empty chairs. She's always making sure we all eat, anyone that enters her kitchen, even me.

Cara moves to sit with Ava, but Bryson grabs the seat next to her first. Cara gives him a dirty look, but he purposely ignores her.

He pushes his chair closer to Ava and leans even closer. "How are you feeling?" he murmurs in her ear almost too silently for me to hear. Ava opens her mouth to reply, but I don't get to hear her response because the girls pull their chairs back and it makes too much noise.

My irritation must be obvious because Tiffany clears her throat and looks down at her hands folded on the table. "Sorry," she mumbles, but I think it's more than bad timing. I think she was trying to hide my daughter's response.

I look at Ava and she seems paler than usual. I thought it might have been the stress of everything that's been going on. We've been through so many changes so quickly, and with the guys being in the hospital on the brink of dying, we've all been sick with worry. "Is your sister okay?" I ask Ezra. He only shrugs and goes back to his phone

Ava and Bryson are murmuring with one another, and with their heads so close together, it's impossible to hear what they're saying.

I mindlessly grab a piece of sausage from my plate and start eating, but my eyes are glued to my daughter's back, trying to put the puzzle together without all of the pieces.

"Wolf." Maybe she has some insight that I'm not quite seeing.

"*Yeah, I got nothing."* My eyes switch to violet.

"But she smells different." I put my nose up in the air and my brows lift. "Hey Ava," I start.

Her head snaps up from her conversation, a hint of panic in her round eyes. "Gotta go, Mom." She stands quickly with the others behind her, and I'm left wondering what just happened? "Don't worry about us..." she smiles over her shoulder as she's nearly out the door. "If you're happy, we're happy." Her voice sounds nervous, but I don't get the chance to ask before the door is swinging shut behind her.

"Love you, Mom," Ezra is the last one to walk out the door, dumping a stack of dishes into the sink before he goes.

"Love you too," I mumble back.

Weird.

Ava's change of scent lingers in my mind all day, and something tells me there's something bigger to blame than a different bottle of perfume. By the time she gets home from work, I still don't get a chance to ask her what's going on. She closes her bedroom door in a hurry, telling me she has a lot of homework she needs to finish by tomorrow.

I sigh and leave her to it. But there's a nagging feeling that there is something I'm not seeing, and I have to talk to her sooner rather than later.

I'll give her space for now, but with Benji and Tyler on the mend and my orders to stay home from work, it's hard not to be obsessed with the small things I may not have noticed before.

The guys tell me not to worry about work, so I have the night to myself and take my wolf out for a run.

Chapter Twenty

Benji

As the doctor suggested, Kat didn't come back last night. So as soon as the sun was up and I could walk properly again, I came straight here. Both doctors wanted me to stay at least another day to fully heal, but I've been kept away from my Kitty Kat far too long.

I try the doorknob and it opens. It's obvious she's not in her room, but her scent is strong, which means she's close. I go to the bathroom and find her starting to undress.

I cross my arms and lean against the door, watching her for a moment, appreciating her smooth, light brown skin and her wolf tattoo peaking off to the side. My wolf and I want to cuddle with her all day and night for the rest of our lives. This woman is it for us. She's our world. The only reason I kept fighting, even when my body was giving out, was to see her again. I was fighting back to her.

"I remember that first day we officially met. I told you, one day you'd ask me to shower with you." She finally undresses and my cock begins to throb. "I just didn't know how soon you'd invite me."

She looks surprised at my arrival. My footsteps are extremely quiet. That's what made us lethal once upon a time, not even other supernaturals would know we were hot on their trail.

She narrows her eyes. She's having an internal debate with herself, but it has nothing to do with having sex and more to do with being afraid of hurting me. "You're not fully healed yet, are you?"

I shrug, turning around slowly so she can take a good look, showing her I'm not too hurt for this. It was hell being in bed and not being near her.

I'm going to have her sleep in my room. I look around, but on second thought, I might sleep in here instead. Her room is cleaner than mine and it smells exactly like Kat. "All I need is you. You're my medicine."

She rolls her eyes at my attempt to be romantic. "Just get in," she snaps and I snicker.

"So demanding my little Kitty Kat." I wrap my arms around her naked body. "I think living with

Alphas has made you dominant." She chuckles at my humor, pulling back and sinking into the tub, her soft naked body begging to be cherished.

"You better get in or I'll change my mind." Her body is already relaxing.

"You won't change your mind," I say with so much confidence and a wink that promises a good time.

She looks back with a dreamy gaze. "I wouldn't?" she says coyly.

Not wanting to test the waters any longer, I take off my clothes with a quickness I didn't know I had in me, throwing them off to the side and immediately stepping in.

"Ouch." The water is fucking hot. "Kat, what the hell? This is the type of burning water they have in hell," I say trying to slowly ease my body to the temperature. "Are you trying to peel off my sensitive skin?"

"Don't be a baby," she huffs, obviously enjoying the water from the depths of hell. "This is perfect." Yeah, perfect for a demon, but I stay quiet, not wanting to give her a reason for telling me to get out.

"I thought I almost lost you," she sighs, putting her head down on the edge of the tub. I walk over to her using my fingers to lift her chin up.

"Hey," I say gently. "I'm here and I'm not going anywhere. I just found you and I'm never letting you go," I murmur against her lips. She may not be my mate, but this is damn close to what I think it would be like.

She leans forward, pressing our lips together and kissing me hungrily. It feels good knowing she wants me as much as I want her. She's everything I never knew I wanted or needed. This is a gift from the goddess herself.

I've done a lot of bad shit in my lifetime, so for me to have someone as special as Kat on my side makes me appreciate how lucky I am.

She pushes further into the kiss, making it known she wants more from this. She pulls back, only a hair's breadth away. "Sit down," she says, power vibrating through her words.

"Woah, Kat. I've never heard you be so commanding. I like this new you." I smirk playfully, knowing it will get a rise out of her. It comes so easy and so natural to be this way with her. I can't believe we've only known each other for a short amount of time.

"Oh hush up, Benji." But her eyes turn down for a moment, hiding her sadness, and I know she's still thinking about my brush with death. I don't want her to hide any part of herself from me, I want to know and see everything about her. I gently lift her chin again and the heat returns to her gaze.

I get up from the water and sit on a small bench inside the tub, and as I move, she slides in between my legs effortlessly. My cock is ready for anything she has on her mind.

She lowers her head, and I can feel her hot breath on my skin. My body stiffens, building the anticipation. The days I was not well, I wanted to be with her so badly. She was the one that kept me going.

Her lips press against my cock and the slight touch has my eyes rolling back. "Shit, wait Kitty Kat don't move." I have to control my body, or I'll explode before she even starts moving. "Okay, I'm ready," I say once I'm calm enough. She adjusts her mouth to my length, and it takes her a moment before opening wider and going deeper.

She hums against my dick, the vibrations have me curling my toes. I fist her hair, guiding her to a speed that won't tip me over just yet. I want to feel more of her.

An unwanted thought crosses my mind of her doing this with other men, and I start to get jealous, but immediately remember she's only been with one. They didn't do much other than sex, but the way she's sucking feels like she's experienced.

I pull her hair up while she licks the tip, swirling her tongue around my sensitive area. "Keep doing that, baby," I growl out. "Your tongue...so good on my dick." I can't form coherent words anymore.

Her eyes light up as she continues to suck, showing me how much she's enjoying this. She lowers her head again, moving up and down in a perfect rhythm. I have no words anymore, I can't think, I can't talk, I can only feel the sensation my girl is giving me.

Sensing someone watching us, I look up, knowing I'll find Az staring at us. His gaze is dark and full of lust and he's holding on to the wall with his knuckles in a tight fist. I look down at my girl's head and back up again, watching the way he adjusts himself in his pants. According to Tyler, he hasn't fucked anyone since Kat showed up, but I know he's been to The Black Rose— the BDSM club he frequents—more than usual lately, taking up space in the darkest corners to watch other's living out their fantasies. Judging by the rapid rise and fall of his chest, maybe he's got a fantasy of his own brewing behind his angry blue eyes.

He watches greedily as Kat's head bobs up and down. I know by now Kat has noticed we have an audience, and I wonder if she's putting on a show for him too. His mouth is slightly parted, and he starts rubbing himself with the palm of his hand.

My balls tighten, and when she realizes I'm getting close, her movements grow erratic, setting a speed that's going to tip me over the edge. My tip pushes against the back of her throat as it starts to swell, her cheeks bulge and she makes sure she takes every last inch of me when I explode in her mouth. I groan loudly as she laps up every single drop of my release. She licks her lips before bringing them close to mine. I bite her plump bottom lip, now tasting my salty cum on them. I like knowing I'm the first dick she's sucked.

I look back but Az is already gone.

When she pulls away, her eyes wander to the door and then back to me. "Don't you ever do that to me again, Benji!" She slaps my chest gently as if it were my fault that I got sick. I can't get upset at her for that. I would be angry and losing my shit if our positions were reversed.

She feels around our bodies until she finds exactly what she's looking for. It's been hard since she sat on top of me, which was only about a minute after I came. She guides me in between her legs. "Wait," I stop her before she pushes down over me. "I need to get you wet first." I don't want to hurt her, especially when I expand.

"Benji, I'm done waiting. I've been wet since you..." She looks down shyly and I bring my hand underneath her chin, nudging her face up again. "You know."

"What was it?" I act confused as she flushes a scarlet shade of red.

"Benji," she sighs. "Are you going to make me say it?"

"Hey, you don't have to be shy about what we did." She nods her head. "I think what you're referring to is the day I licked that sweet pussy of yours," I say next to her ear, and she closes her eyes, shivering, like she remembers exactly what I did to her cunt.

She opens them back up staring at me. "Yeah, when you did that. I've been wet for you ever since." As if to prove her point she slides my dick inside her slick walls. Holding my neck tightly for support.

"I've missed this so much," I say, enjoying the feel of her. It's been too long since we've done this.

"Me too," Kat says, excitement lacing her voice. She moves slowly trying to fit my whole cock inside of her. She tilts her head back while I hold on to her waist. With one hand, I bring her head back and start sucking on her neck. That prompts her to start thrusting.

"Claim her." My body momentarily freezes.

"Are you okay?" she asks in a small voice. Shit, she sensed my hesitation.

"Keep moving, Kat. Don't fucking stop." She looks me in the eyes and smiles wickedly.

She thrusts letting me forget my wolf's voice, like she wants this moment to be ingrained into her memory forever, just in case anything else happens. I won't let anything happen if I can help it. She's mine, and if I could, I'd mark her permanently.

I grab her waist while my other hand travels down to her pretty pink nub. I rub it until she's rolling her hips harder, faster. I lower my head sucking on her tit. Her eyes turn violet before she closes them, savoring the moment.

"Benji, I'm going to come." The next moment she's squeezing me tightly inside her walls while I'm swelling inside of her, and moments later, I come for the second time.

She holds onto me tightly like I will disappear if she lets go. "I'm not going anywhere," I reassure her. No matter how exhausted my body is, and against the doctor's wishes, being here with Kat is worth it. Even when I was sick, if I could have just walked, I'd have made it to her every single night.

I get up from the bench, bringing us back to the scalding heat of the devil's lair, keeping an arm around her. Pumping shampoo into my palm, I work it into a lather and massage her hair. She leans in response and my wolf perks up.

Once I've rinsed the shampoo from her hair, I do the same with the conditioner, keeping a tight arm around her the entire time.

When we're both clean and wrapped in towels, there's a heavy knock on the bathroom door.

"Hurry up and get dressed, I need you guys," Ash says urgently.

We look at each other, bolting out of the bathroom. What's happened now?

Chapter Twenty-one

Kat

I almost run out of my room but my phone rings with a message. It's probably my kids. I walk back to my dresser to pick it up and nearly drop my phone when I read the message.

Jess: We need to talk. It's urgent!

My spine goes rigid. Well, this was unexpected. It's not like I've forgotten about my best friend, but I've had a lot going on this last week. We don't usually go this many days without seeing each other, but my life has changed in a very short amount of time.

The *urgency* in her message has me on edge. What could she want? Did she find out something about me? I should have called her again until she picked up. I should dial her number now, but I don't have time. Can't keep that asshole waiting. Ah, fuck him. I call her but it goes straight to voicemail.

Me: What's going on?

Jess: I can't tell you over the phone. Meet me at my house. I'll be here around six. Any time after.

It's one o'clock, so if I leave around three, I can make it there by six.

My stomach is churning. I have a bad feeling about this. She's not telling me something, and I'm too scared to find out what it is because there is no way she knows what I am. Right?

Jess: It's about who you are.

Shit.

The walls are closing in, I sway back and forth, shutting my eyes tightly before opening them back up. She has information about who I am, possibly about what I am. I try not to let that get me angry, but in the back of my mind, I'm feeling a little betrayed that she's been keeping this from me. But that would be hypocritical because so have I. I've kept this secret for a week now. Jess and I have always depended on each other. I should've told her from the beginning.

"I told you so!" my wolf shouts at me like a nagging parent.

Does she hate me now? Will things change between us? I hope she understands that I'm the same person I used to be. Despite my enhanced wolf abilities and immortality, I'm still the same Kat I've always been. Oh wait, maybe with a slightly bigger appetite, but that's it. Nothing else has changed. Oh wait, I've had sex with two men, given out a blowjob and got my pussy eaten really fucking good. But that's it. That is all. Oh yeah, and the divorce too. Okay, now I'm done, that's definitely all of it.

"Maybe she means your personality and not that you're a shifter. Maybe she means you're a shitty friend for not seeing her sooner, especially after the divorce."

"Mhmmm. You have a point." Maybe I'm just overacting and she really doesn't know anything. I guess there's only one way to find out.

Me: Yeah, I'll meet you tonight

Jess: Can't wait! I've missed you Kat.

Me: I've missed you too amiga

There's a sadness in her words that I can sense through the phone, and that scares me the most.

Before I get dressed, I take a moment to lay on the bed and breathe, staring at the ceiling.

I better go see what Ash came in for that was so urgent. He better have a reason for interrupting us. The only good thing about me going out there, is that Benji will be there. I already miss his closeness. I don't know what it is about these guys wanting to be with them every single moment of every day.

"You're dick whipped." My wolf laughs hysterically.

"I think you mean pussy whipped." I've never heard of dick whipped before.

"Well, for you it's dick whipped." God, this wolf is so annoying.

"I should see if I can get a replacement for you," I huff out.

"You would never." She narrows her eyes at me in mock hurt.

I smile triumphantly. *"Maybe I would."* I say, adding a little shrug, which probably looks strange to someone on the outside. We both know I wouldn't want to trade my wolf. She's a part of me, after all.

I follow the shouts that are going on back and forth. I don't even have to ask where we're meeting up. Sighing, I walk down the stairs where there's a heated debate going on. I could only guess what that's about.

Standing in the dining room, they all stop talking to look at me and then continue as if I'm not even there. I debate whether to stay or leave them to their bickering. I have too much on my mind right now to worry about what's going on.

Tyler and Benji have circles under their eyes, hunched over slightly. I cringe knowing I should have made Benji rest instead of getting down and dirty with him, and Tyler looks like he needs more sleep.

As I turn to leave, not wanting to be a part of this dispute, Ash growls out, "I bet you're happy." My back stiffens and I slowly turn back around, wondering what the hell I did now. His face is stone cold. Blue with green speckled eyes swirling into a rage.

"What did I do now, Ash?" I sigh, my voice lacking its usual bite. I'm getting worn out from his game of blaming me for everything. Him and Az are sitting to my right while Tyler and Benji sit across from them. I move toward the end of the table, choosing not to take a seat. I'm hoping this will be a brief encounter.

"Oh, he hasn't called you yet?" I scrunch my brows and wait for him to talk, but I guess I need to pry the information out of him. It's exactly what he wants, which annoys the shit out of me.

I'm debating whether to continue this conversation. Something is telling me to just walk away, but clearly I haven't learned my lesson about trusting my intuition. "Who hasn't called me?"

"Dante." My eyes widen in surprise.

"We saw him die." I point to him. "You saw him die, too."

He laughs darkly. "This was probably your plan all along." I grab my dark strands, wanting to rip them off my scalp in frustration.

"Come on, man," Tyler interjects. Now I know why they were in a heated argument. "You really think Kat would do something like that?" His voice is tired and weak but he looks more alive than yesterday.

"She wouldn't help Dante in any way," Benji says, looking annoyed that Ash is bringing this shit up.

"So how did you get poisoned?" He stands up and looks at each of us. "Maybe this was her plan all along." My hand twitches wanting to slap Ash across his face for insinuating I was the one who did this. "You were probably poisoned at the club since we know Dante was there. She could have been his accomplice."

What Ash says actually does make a lot of sense. He could have slipped something in his drink. I remember we had one before we started dancing.

But I seriously want nothing to do with that man. "I'm not his accomplice, Ash." Irritation laces every word.

"Shut up, Ash," Benji snaps, crossing his arms angrily. "Kat, we don't think the attack on you and Amara was the council and..." The palms of my hands start to get sweaty. "We have no idea who did it." My breath quickens.

"So, that means someone else is after me? But, why?" I rub my temples. This is becoming too complicated.

“We don’t know,” Tyler answers, putting his elbows on the table. He looks at Ash’s annoyance clear in his eyes. “I wish I was feeling good right now. I’d take you out and beat the shit out of you.”

Az snorts but Ash replies. “Last time was a mere fluke.” Tyler gets out of his chair, bringing his face close to his brother.

“Nah, I beat the shit out of you.” Tyler smirks and winks at me. I shake my head trying not to smile.

“He’s right,” Az responds. “You were out for the whole day.”

“Shut the fuck up, Az.” Ash narrows his eyes at him. Tyler beams before twitching with pain and sits back in his chair.

There’s violence in Ash’s eyes. Trying to bring the conversation back to the task at hand before Ash tries to take him outside and fight when he’s clearly in no condition for that, I say, “Do we know why the council has been quiet?” As soon as those words come out, my hands start to shake, and I turn them into fists so that they won’t notice the panic rising in me. It’s not so much the council wanting to kill me, yeah that part clearly sucks, but the bottom line is my kids. I worry for them.

The tension in the room shifts. It’s so thick you could cut it with a knife. Benji and Tyler sit straighter. Ash sits back down, his posture relaxed, but I know him by now and this is him putting on a show. Az stands up and hides in the shadow.

"Katarina, don't say a word." Ash looks worried, my body now vibrates with nerves.

What's going on? I look around the room for an immediate threat, but I don't find one. What has them so worked up?

I'm about to open my mouth and ask what's going on when Lily comes in with a handsome man wearing a dark suit. "You guys have a visitor," she announces. It's the man's eyes that catch my attention first. They're a deep, vibrant red. The second thing I observe is his smile. He's got the grin of a person who's confident, strolling in this house like he owns the place. Which makes me curious about who the hell he thinks he is and why he's walking in here like he belongs. He's not a werewolf, that's clear.

He's wearing expensive clothing from head to toe. Almost the exact same style as Theo. I recognize the designer now, and that man is practically wrapped in thousands of dollars. His watch alone must be three grand. I've seen Theo wear them too. I think this man and my ex would either get along or hate each other.

"Thank you, Lily," he says as she starts to leave. His voice is deep and strong in a pleasant way, and I wonder if that's how he lures his victims.

"Benji, it's nice to see you looking better." Benji's normal cheeky grin turns into a sour smile. My body immediately tenses up and my wolf sees this newcomer as a threat.

“Tyler,” he says with wide open arms. “That was very generous of you. Lending your brother some of your energy. True brothers indeed.” He talks to them as if they’re old friends, but from the stiff postures of my boyfriends, they’re anything but.

“Ash, I see you’re still grumpy as ever.” He snarls at the man before him, but this new guy doesn’t seem phased by it.

“Aziel,” I immediately go rigid hearing him call him by his actual name. “I see you’re still a rat hiding in the shadows.” The man looks at Az showing his perfect white teeth.

“Glad to see you’re still alive,” Az says in a clipped and bored tone, twirling his knife around his long, strong fingers. I have no doubt he does this to kill at a moment’s notice.

The man has charisma, but if you look closely past all the winning smiles and the expensive clothing and accessories, you can see it’s all for show.

“Here is Katarina,” he says, finally looking at me and walking toward me with arms wide open as if he wants to give me a hug. “Such a beautiful name for a beautiful woman.” He winks secretly like we’re old friends, and all I want to do is run and hide, but I push my shoulders back and stand straighter.

“Get away from her,” Tyler says in a clipped voice. I see the tension in his shoulders.

"Why are you here, Silas?" Az growls out from the safety of his shadows. I really wish I were standing in the same dark corner that he's in right now. I don't want to be exposed to this man. He's dangerous. Unlike the expensively dressed man before me, the men in this house won't act like they like you when they really don't. This man will wine and dine you and then stick a knife in your back when you least expect it, while grinning widely from ear to ear. That's what makes this man before me more dangerous than any other man in this room.

"Well, as you know by law, I can kill Katarina right here and now," he says nonchalantly. A growl wants to come out of my mouth, but I clamp it shut. I watch as Tyler and Benji tense. There's a slight twitch in Ash's eye. I can't see Az very well to see whether or not he's disturbed by this man's words. Likely not. "But it would be such a shame." He looks at me now with a pouty face, and he has the same red stains on his lips that Az does, but he's no wolf. This man is a vampire.

He comes closer, and in the background, I can hear the men yelling out in protest, but I don't quite understand what they're saying. I'm working hard to keep my face neutral because I'm not sure what his angle is, and I'd rather keep my eyes on the threat.

His red eyes remind me of rubies, and when his gaze locks onto my face, I know my own eyes have shifted to violet. He falters slightly, but quickly composes himself like nothing has happened. "So the stories are true," he says, tilting his head, studying me like a rare species he wants to dissect. I hate it.

Something behind me catches my eye, when did Ash get behind Silas? Benji and Tyler are behind him. I briefly look at Az's spot, but he's no longer there. He's moved. I just don't know where, yet.

Someone grabs me from behind, startling me for a quick second before I recognize the black rose tattoos on the backs of Az's hands that are wrapping around my waist and bringing me close to his chest.

"Relax, Az. I didn't come here as a council member." Council? My pulse quickens and Az sniffs me, nuzzling my neck and sending shivers down my back, but it's oddly comforting.

"Then why the fuck are you here?" Ash growls out.

"I'm here with a truce." I already don't like where this is going.

"Many of the people in the council want her dead, but we have been assured she is harmless. Apparently, she doesn't carry the power we thought she would. Her power is dull; she's merely a wolf, nothing more. We've been watching her, and her powers should have manifested by now." They've been watching me? This realization doesn't put me at ease.

The men still look unsure about this revelation. But Ash unclenches his hand like he'll hear him out.

Ash looks at me, and I know he wants to tell me something, but I ignore him since I already know what he's going to say. He wants me not to mention anything about the dagger. Like I would. That will just leave me as the target.

"So..." Silas says, but Ash has his full focus on me. I finally gaze in his direction, and he narrows his eyes into slits and looks like wants to grab me by the neck. I smirk at him, and it only makes him angrier. He pissed me off earlier when he accused me of working with Dan. I'm not feeling particularly friendly with him.

"I'll tell the council I paid you all a visit and saw for myself that Kat is truly just a wolf and that our spies are right, we don't have anything to worry about."

"And in return?" Ash asks, playing with his cigarette.

"When Ava is twenty-one, you'll hand her over to me." My eyes snap back to Silas. What he just said made me forget about the beef I'm having with Ash. Az's arms tense around me.

"Kat, I know what he just said, but we can't kill him. I promise you, if you still want to go through with it, we'll find the perfect place to do it where we won't all become a target," Az murmurs in my ear.

"What the fuck do you want with my daughter?" I say through clenched teeth.

"Have you heard about the curse Katarina?"

"I've heard these guys are cursed." He laughs, startling all of us.

"This curse has nothing to do with you or these fools, but it's about your daughter." That doesn't make any sense. Why would Ava be involved in all of this?

My wolf peaks out, assessing our odds of killing him. "Don't Kat," someone says to me. I'm breathing hard trying to contain myself.

"Say what you mean," Ash blurts out.

"It's about Ava. It's always been about her." There is something in his eyes, hesitancy, or maybe he's frightened. I have no fucking clue, but the answer will always be a solid no.

"That's not happening." Tyler crosses his arms.

"You will need someone to—"

"We said no," Benji cuts him off.

"You need to go," Tyler says, starting to walk toward the door. "You've overstayed your welcome."

Az lets me go as we all walk behind Tyler, and he has no option but to walk with us.

"That's not going to happen," I say with finality as I stand just outside the door.

"Katarina, you're going to need my help in the upcoming years." I don't like the sound of that at all. "My home is always open." He bows to me as he turns to leave.

Once he's gone, I nearly fall back, but someone is already there holding me up. "I need to go talk to Jess." I want to put this whole encounter behind me.

Tyler is the first to respond, looking exhausted. "Right now?"

"Yes." I feel like I'm walking from one disaster to the next. Jess is going to freak out when she hears about all this. She's an overprotective aunt to my kids.

"I'll take her." Fuck! Anyone else but Ash. I don't have the energy to deal with his bullshit.

Sensing my despair, my knight in shiny armor steps up. "I can take her," Tyler volunteers.

"No, you and Benji need another day to recover. Stay here." As much as I want to argue, he's right. They need at least the rest of the day to get back to normal. They're already looking better than they were. Shifter healing is fucking awesome.

They both look like they're about to argue, but I put my hand up to stop them. "I'll go with Ash. You guys stay here." Az is nowhere in sight. He probably left as soon as Silas did, or maybe he followed behind him to make sure he really left.

He takes the keys from his pocket. "Let's go." He walks out without waiting for me.

Well, this should be fun.

Chapter Twenty-two

Ash

I get into the driver side of my pick-up truck, and she gets in on the passenger side. Katarina puts on her seatbelt angrily. I didn't even know that was possible, but she's seething inside, and I know she's about to explode. It's there in her violet eyes. She needs to take out her anger and pain. What Silas said couldn't have been easy to hear. She's scared, and rightfully so. She hasn't had a chance to ease into this whole new life of hers, and yeah, maybe I'm part of the reason why she looks like she's about to murder someone.

As much as Katarina wanted to avoid me at all costs, she wouldn't have taken her anger out on Tyler or Benji. She needs to let it out, to scream or cry. Plus, I meant what I said, they need at least one more day to heal. Az was not an option; they wouldn't have made it out alive. Knowing the strength in Katarina's eyes, she would have gone straight for the blow, and Az doesn't think before he reacts. It would have been a blood bath.

I was the only option since Amara needed a break. I need a distraction anyway, and she's the perfect fit.

Not able to keep her mouth shut any longer, she speaks up. "So you worked for the council, and yet you think I'm working with Dan?" she sneers. "I don't even want to see his fucking face. He turned me into a shifter," she says with disgust, and I flinch like the word tastes sour in her mouth. Ouch!

"What's so wrong with being a shifter?" I snap back defensively. "You get healing abilities, you're stronger and live a longer life than a human, not to mention we're just a better species."

"Nothing is wrong with being a shifter." Her voice raises a couple of notches. "I would have loved to make that decision for myself." She crosses her arms over her chest, and I avert my eyes to keep myself from staring at her breasts.

"Then why do you sound disgusted?" I grind my teeth. Maybe this wasn't such a good idea. Maybe I should change the subject, but for some reason, I can't. I'm looking for a fight too.

"Do us all a favor and just fuck her already. Claim her. She's ours." My wolf stomps around in my head.

"No, she's not fucking ours." I tighten my fist on the steering wheel. I don't know how many times I have to tell my wolf she doesn't belong to us before he gets it.

"I'm not disgusted," she emphasizes. "I'm angry and pissed off at how I was given no warning, Ash." Even while angry, I love hearing her say my name, but the context she's using it in just pisses me off. "I can be angry about this, can't I?"

"Well, Katarina, did someone pay you to get close to us?" She pulls her hair in frustration; she does that a lot. At this rate, she's going to end up bald by next week.

"Really, Ash?" she shouts even louder. "You're the one who worked for the council and probably went on a crazy power trip."

"You have no idea what we did when we were working with the council," I say so harshly that she flinches at my words. I almost feel bad, but rage is the strongest emotion I'm feeling and the only one I want to stay. If I go with caring, then I'd break down, and it wouldn't be fair to Emma, my true mate.

"What did they make you do?" she says quietly as her innocent eyes try to read my face.

I laugh bitterly. "We were trained killers." I smile wide, knowing it looks dark and sinister. Her eyes wander to the door, but she knows she has nowhere to go.

"You want to know what our curse is?"

"What is it?" she says with a hint of fear laced in her voice. Her eyes wander around trying to find an escape, but there is nowhere for her to go where I won't be able to find her. Her scent is ingrained in my memory, and no matter how much I hate being so close, I can't deny the way it draws me in. No matter how much I want it or not. This is the real reason I push her away. My every thought, day and night, is about her. I already know she's not working with Dante, but I almost wish she were, then I'd have a reason to kill her and get her out of my every thought.

"We have magic." Both of her eyebrows lift in shock, but she already knew somehow. She reminds me of the story of the little red riding hood, backing up like I'm the monster who's going to attack her, and maybe I am, maybe she should be afraid. All of our demons are coming out, and nothing good can come from this situation.

"Our magic is bound by the witch." A sudden feeling of cold and heaviness descends upon my body. It's been too long since I've been able to access that part of me. It's like a limb that you can still feel but it's no longer attached to your body. "There's very few shifters that have magic. Ours manifested when we bonded as a pack. We were probably the only hope of killing the witch." Without our powers, Katarina and her dagger may be the only hope now. "So, tell me, Katarina..." My voice is chilling and her scent changes to one of fear. I inhale deeply, loving that scent. It's like the smell of a hunter catching its prey, and it's one of the sweetest smells. "Do you want to know why we're called the Iron Beast Pack?"

Her cheeks redden, not from embarrassment, but from fear. My scent has changed and she smells it too. Her eyes wander to her bag on the floor, and I know she brought the dagger with her.

She swallows hard before answering. "Why?" she stutters, but when her eyes change, I know her wolf has taken over.

"Because we control the iron in blood." Her mouth parts, and I lick my lips watching as she follows the movement. She looks back at me. "What makes us truly dangerous is that we can slow the blood flow in supernatural and human brains." Her scent changes again, no longer of fear but determination, and I know if I were to attack, she'd put up a fight. I close my eyes, willing myself to calm down.

"We've been weakened drastically and there's another part to it that I can't tell you." She frowns because I know she wants to know, but I'm telling her the truth. I can't tell her because the witch won't let me. "Rumor has it, the main guy on the council, the one who pulls all the strings, has someone with violet eyes locked up. Her eyes are wide open. I know she has questions. Lots of them. I raise my hand up. "I honestly don't know what you are. I'm truly sorry." I feel the need to apologize because for a moment she looked hopeful, and I've crushed it. There's nothing worse than wanting to know more about who you are but having no one to ask.

"You said the main guy. I was under the impression they all ruled equally." She bites her bottom lip.

"They're supposed to, but there's one who has been pulling all the strings." She raises her brows in shock.

"How many make up the council?" She watches me carefully.

"There are twelve. Two vampires, shifters, witches, angels, demons, and Fae." She nods her head, pinching her bottom lip with her fingers in thought. "But, like I said, there's only one of them that really rules."

"Have you met—"

"No. He gave the majority of the orders, but we never met him." He remained invisible to the point where my brothers and I believed the other council members made this person up just so we didn't take it out on them when the worst jobs came in. Maybe there really are only eleven.

She leans closer to me. "We can try to get the person out from the council's grip. Maybe the person there can give me more information on who and what I am." Her back straightens with hope.

"Yeah, that would be dangerous." I tell her while she looks out at the passing scenery, the rain beating hard against the window. I stay silent, trying to gather my thoughts.

"I think we may need to. No one deserves to be a prisoner," she mutters.

That word *prisoner* is like a punch to the gut. It's what my brothers and I are to the witch. We stop talking for a while, her hands fidget the whole time.

"You should try being nice to her. She obviously looks worried." My wolf peaks out once again. I look over to Katarina and she is biting her lip really hard, bouncing her knee up and down.

"So… It's a nice day today." My wolf cringes and I want to palm my face.

"Huh?" she asks, confused.

"The weather looks like any other day in Washington, like shit. Ask her about Jess," he prompts.

"How did you meet Jess?" I ask awkwardly.

"See, much better." He goes back into his cave letting me attempt to have a regular human conversation with her.

She plays with the zipper on her sweater before answering. "We met in one of our foster homes. I got there first and a few weeks later she showed up," she says with a small smile. The first genuine smile that she's had since we got in the truck. "She's fucking crazy, doesn't give a shit about the law. We got fake IDs before I met Theo and partied and drank almost every day."

I lift my brows up at the news. "You liked to drink?"

"Yeah, well, don't be so surprised, Ash. I used to party it up," she chuckles. "Only for about six months, though. Then Theo came into my life." She touches the bridge of her nose.

"Have you had fun since then?" I think I already know the answer to that one, but I watch her face contort in thought.

"I think it's more complicated than that, to be honest. When I was with Theo, he loved to take me out to work events. Sometimes it was fun to play dress up and pretend I was someone else, but I never really got to be me when we were together. It wasn't so much the drinking and partying I missed about being a teenager, it was just overwhelming having to live up to someone else's vision of the perfect wife. But you know, since I've been here, I got to have a drink when Benji and I went dancing at the lounge. That's the closest to me I've been in years."

"What does your wild best friend think about Theo?" I'm curious to know if Jess sensed there was something wrong with him, and if she did, why didn't she ever tell Kat.

She makes an O with her lips before answering. "Oh, she hates him!" She puts so much emotion in her words. "She didn't want me to be with him, but by that time I had already gotten pregnant." I think I might actually get along with Jess. I can't wait to meet her.

"So, what is she like?" I want to know more about the person who knows Katarina the best because let's be honest, it wasn't Theo, he didn't know shit about her.

She peers down at her phone frowning, then looks back up. "Sorry, I've been trying to message Jess since we left but she's not replying. She's probably still at work," she says almost like an afterthought. "She's the best friend anybody could ask for. Always in your corner." She looks at me, giving me her full attention, her big brown eyes taking me in. "I actually think you guys would get along well." She tilts her head as if she's assessing me. "Maybe I can plead and beg her to move closer to me. I miss her so much!" she says, hugging herself. "This is the longest we've ever gone without seeing each other."

"Does she know you're a shifter yet?" There is no law about keeping who we are quiet, but if you put the whole supernatural community at risk and fuck it up, the council comes after you, the person you told, and their family. Yes, it's brutal. I know because we've been the council's special task force to handle those situations.

She shakes her head. "No, I haven't told her yet, but I'm not leaving her house without telling her." There's a look of determination there, but there's no hiding the slight fear in her eyes. If her friend doesn't accept her, she will be devastated. I'll do what I can to make the revelation go as smooth as possible. No matter how much I'm an asshole to her, I've seen what she was married to, and I won't let anyone else make her feel like she's not good enough. But, if their friendship is as strong as she says, I'm sure Jess will accept her no matter what.

"I wanted to tell her last week. I was just too scared, but if our positions were reversed, I'd want her to tell me even if it scared the shit out of me." She looks out the window again. "I also have to tell her about Dan so she'll be careful. If he is still alive like you implied, I don't know what he'd do to get closer to me again. I'm sure he wouldn't hurt her, but he's an award-winning manipulator. Though, Jess is never one to take his or anyone else's shit lying down. She'll give him hell if he tries anything, just like always." There it is again, that pang of jealousy at not being in her life earlier. I want to lash out and be the asshole she knows, but I bite my lip hard. Now is not the time.

"Sometimes it was us three that would hang out. I always felt like Theo didn't fit in, or maybe he just didn't want to fit in our world. I still don't see how Dan and Theo's relationship lasted so long. They were complete opposites. One is all about having fun and...kidnapping," she says it as a joke, but it falls flat on her lips. I think that event has traumatized her more than she expected. "Theo is all serious and shit all the time."

"How did you end up going out with him, let alone marrying him?" I had one brief encounter with him, and I still can't picture how she stayed married to the guy for so long.

She lets go of a tired sigh. "Well, I hate to say this, but I think it was that he never took no for an answer. Then I got pregnant, and I think he felt some type of obligation to marry me." She glances back at her phone, her brows creasing before looking back up at the road. "He also provided the lifestyle and family I so deeply craved for myself. I was alone for so long that I just wanted a family, and I thought he provided that."

I need to move the conversation away from her ex-husband before I drive to his house, find him, and kill him on the spot.

My wolf perks up from the lazy position he's in. *"I wouldn't mind a detour."*

"Yeah, I don't think the kids would be too happy about that." It's probably the only reason why I won't do it because I'd feel bad for the kids.

"What's the reason we're meeting Jess today besides you telling her what you are?" I realize I never asked her. She needed to blow off some steam and I did too, so I volunteered to drive. I thought it was because she needed to tell Jess about Silas.

"She said she had something urgent to tell me." She bounces her knee up and down again.

"Well, we're almost there." She hugs herself tighter the way she does when she's anxious.

"Yeah, I can't wait," she says in a small voice, and I don't know if she's worried about what Jess is going to tell her or what she's going to tell Jess, maybe a little of both.

We exit the freeway, driving through a neighborhood not as nice as where Katarina used to live. "Her house is right there." She points to a blue house with a nice garden. "Her car is there," she says excitedly. "Park in her driveway." I do as she asks.

She unbuckles her seatbelt. "Wait," I pull my hand out before letting her open the door. "For peace of mind, let me go in first." She bites her lip wanting to argue, but to my surprise she agrees.

I get out of the car first, and I hear her door closing. She's keeping her distance, which is exactly what I want. Well, almost. I want to ask her if she'll stay in the car, but I know that isn't an option.

I approach the door with her a couple of steps behind, lifting my hand to knock but noticing that it's slightly open. My heart rate picks up. I walk into the house and my body stills while the predator in me comes out. I try to turn around to tell Katarina to go back to the car and lock the doors, but it's like everything happens in slow motion. Katarina pushes me aside, falling to the floor with a shrill scream. "No, Jess, No," she repeats over and over.

Jess' body is lying lifeless on the floor, a pool of blood surrounding her tall frame. Her nails are torn and brittle like she was fighting the attacker. Her face is bruised as well as her knuckles. A knife was punctured through her heart, but there's no sign of the weapon anywhere. The attacker probably took it with them.

I'm stunned, but my body recovers quickly. I try to hold her. "We need to get out of here, Katarina. It's not safe. The killer could be close." Although I feel bad taking her away from her dead friend, she's my responsibility, and I can't leave her here.

"I'm not leaving my best friend here." Her voice cracks and hearing her so vulnerable does something to my heart. She usually keeps her emotions tucked in except when she shows me how much she hates me.

She's kneeling next to Jess' head, avoiding the blood. She touches the heart tattoo that mirrors her friend's and puts her other hand on Jess's. "Sisters, we were sisters, and I wasn't here for you," she says in between sobs.

"Katarina! We need to go!" She stands up and pulls away from me, ripping her dagger out. She tips it slightly and points it near my throat.

I back up one step, she's using that weapon carelessly. Her friend, her best friend, just died. She's not thinking straight, she's breaking apart.

My skin crawls and my vision changes, someone is here.

There's a noise and my eyes fly toward the other side of the living room. "Fuck! Not him again."

Chapter Twenty-three

Kat

"I didn't do this to her. I swear it." Are the first words that come out of Dan's mouth when he enters the living room.

I'm empty, I feel drained. There is no emotion there. I hold my weapon to my side, no longer holding it in front of him.

"We need to go, Katarina," Ash says for the hundredth time. But I don't want to leave her behind. She's going to wake up soon.

I know it.

"I want to be here when she wakes up," I tell him as I stare at my best friend who's been through all of my good and bad times.

Ash's eyes widen. "Love," he says gently, as if I were a fucking child, and it pisses me off. He's never treated me this way. Why is he starting now?

"We're not going anywhere," I snap, eyeing the way Ash watches Dan's every move. I'm too tired to care that he's here and not dead in the woods where he belongs. His days are numbered anyway. "You're acting like she's dead when she's not." Ash swallows as he comes closer to me, still keeping an eye on the other man.

"Katarina sweetheart," he murmurs.

"Don't call her that," Dan growls, and as the two men bicker, I grab something from the floor and tuck it into my pocket before they notice me.

Ash grabs me again, but this time I let him. "Sleep," his voice booms. I try to fight his power, but he's my Alpha now, and I have to listen to what he says, even if I don't want to. I try so hard to fight it. I hear him say it two more times before everything goes dark.

I wake up as he's putting me inside the car, Dan is nowhere in sight. In the back of my mind, I notice that his power didn't keep me asleep for very long. "Let me go, Ash." I fumble with my seatbelt and his hands.

"Katarina, we need to go," he pleads. His eyes are on high alert looking around for any threats. It's dark out, but it's not like it matters anymore.

"Get out of my way." I struggle with his arms but he's stronger than me.

"Where the hell are you going to go?" I see the exhaustion in his eyes. He exerted so much power with that one word. I'll just have to wear him out.

Where am I going? I have no clue. Maybe to a bar so I can drink my problems from existence. Yeah, that sounds like a great plan. Maybe Jess will show up and we can drink and dance together like we used to.

Yes, it sounds like a good plan. I kick Ash in the balls and he immediately goes down. "Fuck! Katarina, that was a low blow." I guess it works on shifters too. Good to know.

I don't stay behind to hear what else he has to say. I run, and the wave of nausea hits me, reminding me of the night I became a shifter, but I push that out of my mind. The rain has finally stopped, my clothes are dry, but I need to find a place to go before it starts back up again.

I look behind me, watching Dan running after me, which only infuriates me more. He's the one that turned me and kept me away from my friend. I would have been able to see her that night at the diner if he hadn't turned me into a shifter, and when I tried to see her the day after my divorce, he fucking kidnapped me.

Something overcomes my body, and I stop, waiting for him to catch up. He hesitates before smiling. I grin too, but it's for an entirely different reason. I'm feeling powerful despite witnessing my friend on the floor.

He grabs my waist and I let him, putting my arms across his neck. "Hey Dan, or should I say Dante?" I hum in his ear. "Which one do you prefer?"

"Kat, your eyes are glowing, they look—beautiful." He stares at me like he's mesmerized by them. I bring my hand up to his cheek and he leans into it, smiling at me like I'm his whole world. His life is at my fingertips.

"Katarina, Katarina," Ash yells from far away, but I don't pay him any attention. All my attention is on the man before me. I keep gazing into his eyes as a lover would do, but none of the feelings that come with being in love. I have him right where I want him.

"Katarina, stop." Ash's voice gets closer and more urgent.

"Go away," I growl out, surprised by how different my voice sounds. My energy feels depleted now and only the adrenaline keeps me going.

"Okay," Dan says in response, and he takes off running in the opposite direction from Ash.

"No, wait, not you!" I yell out, "I'm supposed to kill you."

"Fuck! Katarina, shut up. People are going to hear you." Ash gets close to me. "Your eyes, they're almost glowing." He looks back to where Dan left, and I know he's debating to go after him and end his life once and for all, but he clenches his jaw instead. I take the opportunity to start running again.

"Not again! Katarina, wait!" he shouts. "Let's go home."

"No!" I'm not ready to go home or to tell my kids about losing someone else they loved this soon after their father disowned us. "I need a drink." I start walking again.

"Okay, I know a place where we can have one drink." I roll my eyes. I'll have as many as I want because I'll be damned if another man wants to tell me what I can or can't eat or drink. He ain't the boss of me.

His long legs start moving and I jog to catch up to him

We walk a couple of blocks from here to a secluded area. I'm having doubts that maybe Ash actually wants to kill me, but my nerves calm when a building appears. Hmmm...I've never noticed this place before. I run to the entrance, leaving Ash behind. A man appears right in front of me. "Move," I say, and he happily complies. Good, I thought I was going to have to take him down.

The man I presume is a bouncer looks behind me. "Oh, you're here with the Alpha." I ignore him as I make my way in.

The place is dimly lit. Red and black adorn the walls. "Where the hell am I?"

A body moves close to me and whispers in my ear, "It's a brothel." Well fuck. I immediately turn around and come face to face with a tall man whose soft blue eyes have specks of lime green in them. I stumble back, thinking it's the man from earlier trying to kick me out, but it isn't, and relief washes through me until I remember my best friend is dead.

"So umm..."

I'm saved by Ash. "We're here to get a drink, Leo." He puts a hand on the man's shoulder.

"Such a beauty this one." He eyes me up and down. Ash stiffens.

"We came here to have a drink."

"Of course," he says. "Let me walk you two to the bar." I look around the place with its sinful colors. The area I'm currently in is a lounge where lots of people are talking amongst each other with alcohol in their hands. They're sitting on fancy couches that look like they belong in the Victorian era, with layers of sheer fabric and lace hanging from the ceiling. There's a grand staircase near the bar that leads to a second story, and I'm assuming those rooms are where they do the deed. I can smell everyone's arousal. I try to keep my eyes from lingering on anyone too much. Ash's hands go around my waist, what would normally have me shivering with pleasure is making me feel numb now.

"Order anything you want—on the house," the man offers.

Ash leans into him whispering something in his ear, and he nods his head. "I'll bring you a special drink my dear." He winks at me before leaving, and alarm bells go off in my head, but I'm too numb to care.

I look at the people around me flirting and smiling with one another, not really what I want to see at this moment. I look to my left and Ash is staring at me with his blue-green eyes. Ugh there's no other place to look but at the bartender.

"Hey sugar, are you here for a good time," a woman says huskily.

I whip around with a scowl in place. "He's not here for you. Leave him alone." She looks like she wants to argue but only smiles at me and leaves.

Weird.

This place gives me the creeps. The faster I get drunk the better.

The bartender comes back with two shots. It looks like water. I grab mine and take a whiff, while

Ash takes out a cigarette and lights it up. "I'm going to be pissed if this is water."

I look at Ash for a response, but he's too busy lighting up his cig. I smell it again and pull it away from my nose. That's definitely alcohol. I don't care what it is as long as it'll make me drunk and numb. But before I can throw it back, I look at Ash. "Can you message my kids? Tell them I love them and goodnight." I don't want to message them because they'll be asking questions I am not ready to answer.

"Already taken care of." He puffs out a cloud of smoke.

I down the drink and nearly fall out of my chair as it settles in my stomach.

"What the fuck was that?" I slur my words.

"I thought you didn't care as long as you were numb?" I shrug. He has a point. "Another one," he yells to the bartender, and I debate whether to put a stop to this but decide to go through with it. I watch him as he takes his.

Another one is set in front of me, but when I try to grab it, my arms, eyes, and brain aren't communicating the right way. After many failed attempts I finally grab it and put it to my lips, pouring the liquid down my throat.

I touch my face, so far passed feeling numb. The thought of Jess and how I found her is long gone, replaced by a euphoria. I have another drink in my hand. "Drink it," Ash says, and he helps slip the contents past my lips as my hand falters. I look around and we're both sitting on a lavish couch. How the hell did we get here? I don't remember getting up from the bar.

There are people all around us, but between the low lights, the liquor, and the thin layers of lace that separate the seating areas, I can't really make out their faces. "Are they—" My words don't come out the right way, I'm slurring so badly, but I try again. "Are they...having sex?"

"Yes."

"Weren't you just smoking a cigarette?" He looks at his pack.

"I've smoked six already." He's lying. Isn't he?

Stunned, I say, "Where did you go?"

"I've been by your side the whole time." How the hell did I miss him smoking so much?

I close my eyes for a second, swaying to the rhythm of the music, and when I open them again, I'm sitting on top of Ash with his cigarette on my lips as he nips at my neck.

I grind my hips and he groans in my ear, "Is this numb enough for you?"

I have no clue what he's talking about, so I keep my mouth on the cigarette. He takes it back and inhales, moving close to my lips and exhaling into my mouth. I hold it in and let out the cloud of smoke slowly. I have no idea what this is, but I know it's not his usual smokes. This makes me feel a certain way, maybe more relaxed. So numb and relaxed, just the combination I was looking for. But, what for? Does it matter? No, nothing matters but the vibrations of the bass and the way Ash's fingertips leave goosebumps as they trail over my skin gently.

Chapter Twenty-four

Ash

As I lean back on the couch and take another hit of Leo's special blend, my mind and body begin to relax. Katarina's eyes flutter open and shut in the dim club lights as she rolls her head to the same rhythm her hips have found. Strands of her long dark hair drag over my forearm, sending shivers of excitement down my spine. I trail the tips of my fingers up and down the bare skin of her side as her top rides higher, tempting me to take more than I should. No one would discern her moans or mine from any other. We're no different than anyone else coming here to escape their reality.

I weave my fingers through the back of her hair, pulling her closer and using my grip to tilt her head back. She gasps at the feel of my nails on her scalp, and I blow another puff of smoke past those perfectly parted lips. She inhales deeply, and I thrust my hips up, rocking her into me and letting my lips graze hers. This shouldn't be happening, not because I don't want to claim every inch of her, but because she isn't mine to claim. When I nip her bottom lip, she opens slightly, giving me the access I've been dreaming of since the first time she let me kiss her in my office.

She's not in the right state of mind to tell me to fuck off, to push me away in disgust like I fear she would, but I move against her, so soft and tender, the way I crave to hold a mate. The smoke and the liquor hit me all at once, and for the first time in my life, I feel fully at ease. I know the Seduction House has a unique sexual energy that's hard to ignore, but with Katarina riding my lap to the pulse of the music, I never want to go back to the real world, there's only pain waiting for me there.

She arches her back and leans forward, digging her nails into the leather behind my head, her soft panting like fire against my neck. I drop the remainder of my joint into an empty glass on the end table next to the couch, using both hands to grip her round ass as she pushes it out, practically begging me to rip her fucking clothes off. This feels so right.

She fists my hair, grinding faster as my length hardens between us. She's lost in her own world, and when she sinks her teeth into the sensitive skin on my neck, I let out a long groan, tugging the button on her jeans open, so desperate for more of her.

My heart is thundering inside my chest, scared she's going to stop me, but even more afraid that she won't. She needs to tell me no, push me away. Maybe she doesn't realize it's me beneath her anymore, maybe she's so far gone that she thinks I'm Tyler or Benji. My hands pause as I'm dragging her pants over the curve of her ass, the thought of her pretending I'm someone else feels like a bucket of ice water over my head. After everything I've said and done, she couldn't possibly want me.

Feeling my hands fall away from her, Katarina's body slows. She leans her head against my shoulder and moans, "Don't stop, Ash, please."

And I'll be damned if my name on her lips isn't the best fucking thing I've ever heard. "You want this baby?" I murmur in her ear, biting hard on her earlobe. She yelps and shudders against me. "Then say it."

"I want this," she moans softly as my hands find her bare ass once more, pulling her down harder against me.

"You want what?" Her eyes flutter open, landing on my face, watching the fear and the lust warring behind my eyes.

"You, Ash. I've always wanted you." I groan at her words and the smallest smile reaches her lips before I'm grabbing her jaw and pulling her mouth back into mine. When we break for air, I see one of my beta's, Carter, over her shoulder at the bar watching us, and something sours in my stomach as reality knocks a little sooner than I'd hoped.

Her thin hand is pushing past the zipper of my pants, and I grab her wrist gently, shaking my head. She looks crushed for a moment, and when I drag her jeans back up, her hips still. "Not here. Not like this."

Her brows crease in frustration, and I know she must feel like I'm playing a game with her, baiting her in just to turn her down. "I'm sorry, were you too close to feeling something in that cold fucking heart of yours?" Her words slur a little, but her anger is crystal clear.

Carter pushes away from the bar and jerks his chin toward the back door, and as my normal mask of indifference falls into place, Katarina jumps from my lap like I've burned her. When she turns to run, I panic, my hand snapping out and fisting the back of her shirt. "No more running." I seethe, tired of her flighty, defiant bullshit when she doesn't get her way.

Her steps falter, the fairy drops still running their course, and I catch her against my chest, locking one arm around her and grabbing her throat lightly. "Just to be clear, when I take you, I want you to remember every vivid detail of what it's like to have me fuck you—because I won't be able to forget it or walk away like it didn't fucking happen." She inhales sharply, and I drop my hand from her throat. She doesn't say anything, just stares at my back as I head toward the door of the club and signal Carter to be sure she gets to the car safely.

Once I hit the alley, I bypass the waiting car and shift into my wolf, not even bothering to take my clothes off first. I need air. Room to breathe. Space to run until I can't smell her fucking arousal anymore. She just lost her best fucking friend on top of everything else she's been through. I've come to love being the outlet for all Katarina's anger, but I can't live with being another one of her regrets.

Chapter Twenty-five

Az

It's already noon and Kat and Ash still haven't woken up yet. I'm sitting in my bed going over my notes. I have a tight hold on my papers, but all I want to do is throw them at the wall. I'm so frustrated I haven't fucked, which has me on edge. I'm so close to finding that bitch who ruined our lives I can almost taste it, and when I get my hands on her, it won't be pretty.

There's a soft knock on the door. I'm already angry and pissed off, and I need to let go of my pent-up frustration. Maybe I should go back to The Black Rose, maybe this time I'll make it past the bar and find someone to fuck until I can think clearly. I've been there countless times since Kat showed up, wasting my time in the shadows because no one captures my attention. My body doesn't seem to respond to women anymore, but without sex, there's nothing to get my thoughts away from all of the blood and murder. I punch my bed angrily before getting up.

I open the door harshly, already knowing who's on the other side of it. I can practically smell her scent in every corner of my home.

I know what happened to her best friend, Ash told us last night before he passed out. Though a sober Kat would have my head if she knew I sent her kids to stay with their friends overnight, I just had a gut feeling that Kat was going to need some space when she got home. I just didn't know they were going to spend the evening at a brothel getting fucked up. I'm not looking forward to the conversation that needs to take place with her kids, it seems like they were all close.

She looks like she's been to hell and back, slouching against my door frame with big bags under her eyes. I should mind my manners, but instead, I pull the little brat into my room, pinning her against the wall and choking her—not tight enough to kill, but enough to make it harder for her to breathe. My claws slide out, puncturing her neck on each side of her throat. "What are you doing here, Kat?" I growl in her ear, my dick already hardening. I'm stressed about not being able to fuck, and I'm stressed I can't find the witch, and I'm stressed that Kat makes me feel all these emotions that I don't want to have.

My wolf watches in fascination through another lens. He wants to mate with her, wants to make her ours and keep her to ourselves. I'm not so sure that's even possible with someone that isn't your true mate. I push my wolf to the side before he does something we'll both regret like whisper sweet words in her ear.

When she doesn't answer I say, "I should put you over my lap and punish you for coming in here when I told you to stay away from me." She gasps, but there's a twinkle in her eye.

Does she like it rough?

Not the reaction I thought I'd get. I still smile wickedly, but the only thing I see is the heat in her eyes. I move even closer to her, her hot breath touching my neck. I want to say that I hate it, but instead I lick the blood pooling around my fingers. I move even closer to her, dipping my head to catch her familiar scent of cherries, but there's a strange hint of tobacco and cedar, and my eyes snap up to hers, watching a cocky smile take over her shocked face. She reeks of Ash, he's all over every inch of her, and I can't help but wonder what part of the story he left out last night. Her hot breath fans across my neck, and I want to say that I hate it, but instead, I lick the blood from her neck that's pooling around my fingers.

Blood to me can either be violent or sexual, and in this case, it's the latter. She closes her eyes and groans and then I claim her mouth, tasting her for the very first time. The metallic taste swirling around our lips heightens my awareness of how close we're pressed up against one another. I pull away. "And then I should fuck your little cunt for thinking you can come in here when I specifically told you to stay out of my way." I spit out, but my tone doesn't have its usual bite.

She came here for a reason and that's to forget about her feelings and to be controlled. She's gotten a glimpse of what I could offer her. She wants me to control her body and let loose, even if it's just for a little while. I suck in a breath before deciding I can oblige.

With my other hand, I tuck three fingers in between her waistband and push her panties to the side, sliding them in between her folds. Her panties are already soaked, she came here for a reason, and she knows that I'll give her what she wants. The smell of lust assaulted my nose the minute she stood outside. My cock throbs in my pants, ready to be let free and fuck my girl—I mean Kat.

Now it's her turn to take in a sharp breath as I play with her nub. My hand on her neck keeps her in place. I brush my lips against hers when she bites the bottom of my mouth hard enough to draw blood. Instead of getting angry, it excites me, both of us tasting each other's blood.

"She's fucking ours," my wolf hums, but I keep quiet because being with Kat feels so right.

My fingers are coated with her sweet liquid when I pull them out and bring them to her face. "Lick my fingers clean," I command. She still can't move an inch, pressed against the wall. She bites her bottom lip and sticks out her tongue, licking my fingers like a good girl. She's tasting herself and fuck, she looks so sexy sucking them clean.

The smell of her arousal is thick, and as she throws her head back and closes her eyes, I slip my fingers back into her core. She watches me with hooded eyes as I bring them back to my mouth, savoring each and every single one of my digits. She tastes sweeter than anything I've ever had before.

I let go of her throat, and though she's healing quickly, a single trickle of blood still pours down her neck. I rip the buttons on her shirt open with my bare hands and watch as the blood trickles down her breast. I take one of her brown nipples, shining red, and hover over it before sucking. Wondering if my next words will scare her away. "You're a little slut, coming in here smelling like sex with my brother's scent all over you. Tell me, did you let Ash in this tight little cunt of yours last night?" Her stare hits the floor and I know I've struck a nerve. "What's the matter? Did he leave you high and dry and now you want me to finish the job?"

She looks away, and for a moment there's a tightness in my chest before she responds. "Yeah." Her voice breathy as I bite hard on the side of her breast, drawing more blood. Instead of pulling away like I thought she would, she brings her tits closer to my face. "I'm your little brat..." Her voice is husky as she uses the nickname I gave her, pleasing me further. "And I want you to fuck me." I smile with satisfaction. That's what I want to hear. It pleases me to hear those words coming out of her blood-stained lips.

I let go of her, pushing her closer to the bed and letting my eyes rake over her partially exposed breasts. "Strip," I demand, and though she hesitates, she doesn't disappoint. I've imagined this moment so many times, yet here she is, in my bedroom, peeling out of her tattered shirt and watching me with heated eyes.

I think about the contents of my closet as her clothes fall to the floor. A pretty set of crimson ropes would look beautiful wrapped around her every curve, but my body moves toward her instead. I drag my teeth across my bottom lip, and my eyes refuse to move from the sight before me. "All of it," I spit, motioning downward.

She looks around my bedroom, all her bratty bravado seeming to fall away when she's standing in front of me. She lifts her arms up like she wants to cover the beautiful body that belongs to me—well, for the duration of our time together. "Look at me my little brat." At my order, she drags her eyes from the door and meets my heated gaze. Her posture shifts as she brings her arms back down, and her confidence returns once again. She unbuttons her pants slowly while keeping her eyes on me, kicking them off to the side. The red panties she's wearing are all that's left, and I'm wondering if she wore them for my benefit because she knows how much I like the color.

I almost want to tell her to leave them on because seeing her in that shade exhilarates me, but I'd rather have her completely naked on my bed. She takes them off ever so slowly, keeping me on my toes.

She's such a tease.

When they're finally off to the side. I'm sitting on the edge of my bed not really sure when I got here, appreciating her sexy body. "Come," I instruct, and she answers right away.

She walks over to me, and if the wetness dripping down her thighs is any indication, she likes giving up a small part of her control. "Kneel." She does as I say without complaint. She's perfect as if she's the person I've been waiting for my whole life. When she's down on her knees, I unbutton my shirt and watch as she drags her eyes through every button.

I take it off and throw it on the floor. She takes me in from her position, studying all my tattoos, and her lips part when she finally meets my eyes. "Take off my pants." I stand up to make it easier on her. She tugs on my button and my zipper, and my cock springs free from the confinement it was in.

She pulls them all the way down along with my boxers, licking her lips as she sets her sights on my throbbing cock before her. "You have a piercing and a tattoo." She swallows hard, practically salivating. It's a web that surrounds a violet rose tattoo. I'm so glad I did it because watching how much she wants it is thrilling.

I fist her long dark hair with one tattooed hand, and she yelps at how hard I'm holding on to it. I have her look at me from her position on the bed while I stare down at her. "Do you deserve my cock?" She tries to look down at it, but I keep her head in place with a confident smile, easily falling into the role of her Dom.

"Yes," she says so low that if I wasn't a shifter, I wouldn't have been able to hear it. I can see it in her dreamy gaze that she wants to suck me off, and I want her to do it.

I relax my hold and she moves her mouth down to face it, and the way she's looking at my dick like she wants to devour me for desert has my body reacting all on its own. Pushing my hips closer to her face, I tease her, running the tip of my cock along her parted lips. "I'll tell you what, you pleased me earlier, so I'll give you a taste."

She licks me once and I nearly shudder with need. Fuck, it's been too long since I've been able to finish with anyone. She uses her tongue to move my prince albert piercing, giving it a few more licks before she opens her mouth and closes her eyes. No, that won't do. "Open them." I demand, yanking her luscious strands. I need to see her eyes while she tastes my cock for the first time.

She presses her lips against my length and all I can do is growl like the wild animal that I am. She's got the plumpest lips to suck dick. She expertly knows how to move with the metal bar hanging from the tip. Thoughts fill my mind from when she was doing this to Benji. I wanted her so badly then, but I kept pushing her away. I'm filled with so much need now that I don't have the willpower to let her go, and by the way she's hugging my cock, there's no way I'd let her leave anyway.

I grab her tit, dreaming of what it feels like to slide up and down between her lush breasts.

Her head bobs and my shaft starts to expand in her mouth, she's trying to adjust to its new size, sucking every bit of it like the slut she is.

Before I know it, I'm shooting my seed down the back of her throat, and she milks every last drop. "Good little brat," I say, and that brings a smile to her face. "Now get up and lay on my bed." She does as she's told while I go to my closet.

As I look back at her briefly, she lifts her head with curiosity to see what I've got hidden here. I bet she tried opening this closet when she came into the room and has been dying to see what's inside.

Her greedy eyes take in everything from floggers and wooden paddles, to belts and butt plugs. I eye that one for a moment and look back at her. She's not ready for it, but I will get her to that point.

I smile mischievously when I see the cuffs. They were in my room the day she came in. "Tell me my little brat, when you were snooping through my room, did you notice the cuffs?"

She's having an internal struggle with herself before she answers. "Yeah, I saw them." She looks away to the door briefly so that I can't see what she's thinking, but I know what she wants. She's ready.

"Do you want me to use them on you?" I walk to her, bringing her gaze back to me. She bites her blood-stained lips, contemplating my offer before giving me a small nod.

I get up from the bed and go back to my closet, grabbing two pairs of cuffs and a red and black flogger. I grab both of her delicate hands and restrain her, one wrist to each side of the bed. Her heartbeat pounds rapidly, but it's not from fear, it's from excitement.

"One more thing, little brat." I walk to my drawers, grab a red blindfold, and place it in front of her to see if she'll complain. But there's nothing but determination in her brown eyes. She's given herself completely to me and that excites me more than it should. "If at any time you don't like something, I want you to say red and I'll stop. If I ask you how you're doing and you say green, I'll keep going. Do you understand?"

"Yes," she says. I bring the flogger down inside of her thigh. "Ahh..." she yelps loudly.

"It's yes sir to you. My little brat. Understood?"

"Yes, sir," she blurts without hesitation, which is exactly what I'm looking for.

"Good...good." I pet her hair and she leans into my touch. "Tell me my little brat, has anybody else tasted this sweet pussy of yours?" She gasps, like she didn't think I'd be bold enough to ask this question. "If you don't answer me, I'll bring it back."

"Only Benji and Tyler," she answers almost immediately.

"And no other lovers?" I shouldn't demand this of her, I know she was married for a long time, but I have to know. If only to quiet the raging thoughts going through my head.

She shakes her head but thinks better of it, answering out loud instead. "No." And because she doesn't say sir at the end, I bring it down on her other thigh with a loud crack. Her gasp sends a shiver through me.

"No, sir," she corrects herself.

"Good little brat. Let's hope you learn, or there'll be more punishments than pleasure." I run my finger up and down her sweet cunt. I get close to her ear and whisper, "I'm going to devour your pussy now." Her body shivers while I lean back, settling in between her thighs.

That's all I need to hear before sticking out my tongue and running it across her slick folds. She lifts her hips off the bed moaning. She wants to forget her problems for a while, and I can provide that for her. I need a distraction too.

I can't get enough of her. I want her underneath me, to possess her, and those thoughts scare me. I want her to be mine. I've never had these thoughts with another woman. What is it with this little brat getting my attention? I shouldn't want her.

I grab her breast, rolling the nipple through my fingers, pinching it harder. Her sweet screams, the combination of pleasure and pain bringing her to climax.

I'm almost jealous that Tyler and Benji got to taste her first. "*Well, if you weren't such an asshole, she probably would have come to you first,*" come the unwanted thoughts.

After she comes, I slam my cock into her tight, wet cunt. She wasn't expecting it. Her moans are loud.

She tries to thrust against me, but I lift her hips up and smack her ass. "I'm in control of my little brat and don't you forget it."

"Fuck you," she responds. I immediately stop and lean to grab my flogger. "Sir," she immediately says. But she isn't getting away with this. I pull out and she whines, the desire to thrust back into her is strong, but she needs to learn a lesson.

I bring it back down on her again and lean in to take off the blindfolds. "Who's in control?"

She narrows her eyes angrily. I bring it down on her thigh again, not once, but twice, and the last time more forceful than the first, creating red marks on her skin that I trail over gently using the black and red leather. She winces in pain, but she still doesn't answer me. So I do it to her other side, only harder than I had before. She takes a sharp breath.

"Just fuck me, Az," she yells out in frustration.

"Wrong answer, brat." She's playing with me, trying to see how far she can push me, but most of all, she wants the pain.

So I walk over and undo her cuffs. "I guess I'll be teaching you a lesson instead." She mumbles something incoherent, and when I look at her, she gives me a haughty smile that I return with my own devilish smirk. She straightens up with a slight fear in her eyes, but she knows what to say if it becomes too much for her.

"Upper body on the corner of the bed, I want your ass to hang out." She does as she's told. The supple strips trail down her back, and when she least expects it, I flick my wrist and bring it down on her butt. She yelps and moves. "No moving brat, stand still and take your punishment. All you had to do was listen to me and I would've given you another orgasm, but you chose to be a brat, and so now there will be pain instead of pleasure."

Another two come down over her ass and it's starting to get pink, but I want it to look bright red. I want her to struggle to sit. I want her to remember what we did here, and most of all, I want her to not forget who's in charge. I flick my wrist again and she whimpers. "What's the color my little brat?"

"Green—Sir," she moans, pleasure evident in her voice as the pain provides her with endorphins.

"Now, we're going to try this again, and if you don't behave well...I'll grab the butt plug instead." She breathes hard. "Oh, we'll be getting to that, just not today." I bring the flogger down hard against her ass and watch her legs quiver as she suppresses a scream. *Good girl.* Using my free hand, I push two fingers deep into her slick core, and she hugs them so tight that I slip right out.

Dropping the flogger to the floor, I shove her onto my bed, grab her hips, and push them out, guiding my cock back inside her gushing pussy.

Welts of blood form where I brought the flogger down. My claws trace one of the harsh lines and red liquid starts to pool from it. She gasps. “Color, brat?”

“Green, sir.” Her voice is husky and I do the same to the other side. I use the blood to rub around her tight round bottom.

“Fuck, Sir! I’ve never experienced anything like this.” Her voice is breathy. I can’t help but feel cocky right now. “You’re going to make me come,” she screams. “I want this to last forever.” I know exactly what she means. I need this too. I’ve been sexually frustrated, and no one has been able to satisfy me until this brat. I don’t want it to end either.

“I’m almost there, sir,” she pants.

I grab her hair pushing up toward the mirror in front of us, her violet eyes stare into my amber one’s. I want to see her eyes while we fuck. I want to see her face as I take her pussy. I want her to see who is fucking her and to never forget it.

“Come for me my little brat.” A few more pumps and I start to expand, she groans so loudly that if our walls weren’t soundproof, everyone would have heard her. My seed spills into her while her walls squeeze me tightly like she’s branding me as she’s chasing her orgasm.

I’m spent, I haven’t climaxed like this in a very long time. Actually, come to think of it, I don’t think it's ever felt this good. I get off of her and grab a towel from my closet, using it to wipe her down.

Her brown eyes gaze up at me. She's flushed and I have to hold on to those cuffs tightly. All I want to do is put them back on her and see what else we can do. Maybe finally stretch her ass. I don't think anyone has gotten in there and I want to be her first. I'm feeling possessive and if one of my brother's takes it before I do, we'll have a fight on our hands.

"How do you feel?" I ask as we both sit on the edge of the bed. She winces. I grab her hair and push it back, playing with her long strands.

I don't know what she sees in my face, but her eyes widen. "I have to go clean up," she says, quickly getting up from the bed and running to the door, leaving her clothes behind.

Probably a good thing she left. I would have tried to fuck her again.

Chapter Twenty-six

Kat

I don't want to admit it, but what Az and I did opened another potential heartbreak. He's the one I thought I would never have anything with. I was so sure about it, and now I'm like putty when it comes to all of these men.

I wanted an escape, I wanted to get away before I read the letter, and I knew he could provide that for me. I knew he'd make me forget even if it was only for a little while. I trusted him enough not to hurt me. I trusted him to care for me, and he didn't disappoint. Being with him was another level.

I gave him both my mind and body to do with it as he wished, and he did what I wanted, even when I couldn't say it out loud. It's like our bodies and our wolves are so in sync, it's almost scary. I've never experienced this type of vulnerability with anyone before. He looked deep into my soul, where no one should ever look because it shows them your deepest secrets and darkest desires, and I'm not sure if I can trust Az that way. He has his own secrets, and he's really good at hiding them.

After a while of hiding in my room, I decide to come downstairs to get some water. After what we did, I need something to hydrate. I eye the bag of chips in the pantry and shrug, not caring that there's no nutrition when I notice Az's red button up. It's just sitting on one of the chairs. Asking—or better yet, begging—for me to take it.

"It's like he left it there for us to take," my wolf says.

My greedy eyes take in that red button up just sitting over the chair waiting for me to grab it and keep it with the rest of my stash.

I look around to see if anyone is near before I raise my head up high and sniff the air, then I listen closely, but no one seems to be around.

I walk closer until I'm standing right in front of where it hangs, taunting me. "Maybe we should leave it here," I tell her. *"I think he'll come looking for it."*

"Unless he left it for us to take."

"Mhmmm..." I can't disagree with her. My hand hovers over it, begging for me to snatch it and take it with me.

I tilt my head to the side, assessing my surroundings to make sure this is not a trap. My wolf is on edge waiting for me to pick it up.

My heart is pounding so loud, I'm afraid it will attract an audience.

Maybe I should leave it but... No, I have to have it. It's mine. I grab the shirt before I change my mind and carry it all the way upstairs. I don't want anyone to catch me with it. I'm sure he won't miss it. He has a lot of them at his disposal, he won't miss this one.

I slam my door shut, inhaling the smell of Jasmine, Nutmeg, Ginger, Lavender & leather. Az's smell. Although I'm still confused about what to think about him, his smell is so irresistible to me. I'm drawn to him like a moth to a flame. My wolf stirs waiting for me to put it up to my nose and inhale his manly scent. Unlike my human side, my wolf has claimed him the minute they've met.

I sit down on my bed and wince. I'm almost completely healed but my butt is still a little sore. I'm surrounded by the collection of the guys' clothing. I set my chips on Tyler's hoodie and grab the note I managed to take before I left Jess's place. My heart mourns for my friend. I should have seen her earlier. I should have demanded a car to get to my best friend sooner. What kind of friend am I? I got caught up with all the guys that I forgot the person who has had my back for a long time.

She dated the letter two days ago, and I wonder if she had worked on it that long. I hold on to the paper tightly, afraid of letting it go, but also afraid of reading her very last words, knowing I'll never hear from her again.

Hey Kat. If you're reading this letter, it means I'm dead.

Shivers run down my body, and my eyes burn with unshed tears. It's only a matter of time before they start falling freely. Fuck! I don't know if I can go through with this. Maybe I should call one of the guys to read it for me.

No, I have to do this myself.

This is the last time Jess and I will spend a moment to ourselves, just me and her. I want to cherish this moment. I wipe the tears away with my sweatshirt before continuing.

What I'm going to tell you is not going to be easy, but our stories have never been easy.

She's right about that, they sure haven't been. We've been through a lot together. This is the moment I realize that I'm truly alone. The person I always relied on is not here to comfort me, to make me laugh, to cry alongside me. This hurts so deeply down to my bones, and the pain weaves its way to my broken heart.

"Keep reading." My wolf's voice is gentle. I've yet to hear her speak in this tone, she's always snarky and rude. Hearing her speak this way almost makes

me break into a sob again, the way I did when I first saw Jess de... When I went to her house last night.

I look down again.

I was really hoping to be there with you and hold you while I told you the full story. My biggest regret in life is that I had to lie to you.

I can almost see her unnaturally light blue eyes, which have always seemed so strange to me, but the color complimented her face so perfectly, no one but her could ever look good with that color. Maybe I'm biased because she is—was—my best friend. Talking about her in the past is going to take some getting used to. This all still feels like a nightmare that I'll be waking up from soon, and when I wake up, I'll talk to her about it, and she'll calm me down and come visit me. She'll come and hug me, kiss me, and be the good friend she's always been.

By now you already know about the supernatural world.

I should have gone to her when I had the chance. My wolf even told me to tell her about what I'd been through, but I pushed back thinking my friend would lose her shit. I didn't give her enough credit, and that will always be one of my biggest regrets. But I also can't help but wonder why she kept the supernatural world from me. Did she think I wouldn't be able to handle it well?

I wanted to be the one to break it to you. What happened to you, it wasn't supposed to happen this way. You were supposed to have a better life than your family.

I crease my brows in confusion. *My family?*

I have lived a very long time.

I wonder how long she was alive. Is she older than the guys? Why was she living in my foster home? I wish she were still alive to ask her the questions that are running rampant through my mind.

You have power, Kat.

My whole body vibrates as if the power she's talking about is awakening again. I look at the dagger sitting on my nightstand and can see it almost shaking in place. I go back to my letter.

I was always trying to hide it, but it kept coming back and becoming stronger and stronger until there was no way I could actually hide it from you or anyone else anymore, so I did the unthinkable.

Oh no, Jess what did you do? What did you do to me? My mind flashes back to when we were sixteen... Well, when I was sixteen, who knows how old she was. Something happened and I felt something change.

I am so sorry, Kat. I tried to protect you, so I hid it the only way I knew how. He was always a danger to you. I should have known.

Who is she talking about? Dan? It has to be. She probably knew Dan was supernatural, and maybe she knew what he wanted to do to me all along and she wanted to shield me from him.

I loved you so much, Kat. All I wanted to do was protect you and the kids. The kids meant the world to me. I loved them like they were my own.

Oh God, I can't read anymore; my heart can't take it.

I stand up from the bed pushing aside the pile of clothing, I need some fresh air. I open the window beside my vanity table and take a moment, breathing in and out. The cool crisp air breezes into my room. "Oh Jess, you would have loved it here." I say out loud as I watch the pool from my window. I smile slightly, remembering one summer when we broke into a rich couple's home while they went on vacation and used their pool. We nearly got caught too, but we were too skilled at not being seen. I rest my elbow against the window seal. Or maybe it was whatever magic she had in her that prevented us from getting caught. I wish I knew what type of supernatural she was.

When I'm calm enough again, I sit back down and grab the clothing, holding my items against my stomach.

If anything happened to you, I would have taken them from Theo.

I know she would have done anything in her power to take them away from him. She's never liked him.

We are always there for each other. There isn't anyone like you and there will never be anyone like you.

I'm starting to wonder if there was something more? Something I wasn't seeing that was always in front of me. It hurts that I won't ever be able to ask what she meant.

As much as I wanted to tell you, Kat you have to understand, I was bound not to say a word. It killed me, but now that you're a shifter, things have changed. I waited for you to approach me. I didn't want to spook you. I wanted you to come seek me when the time was right.

I sigh because I sought her out too late. Maybe things would have been different if I met with her earlier. Maybe even the day I came home from being abducted by Dan.

I don't know if I can read more of this. It's too raw, and after seeing her on the floor. I sigh thinking about leaving her there and not giving her a proper burial. We should have taken her with us, but Ash insisted we needed to go.

I need to ask the guys what happened to her body. I close my eyes while tears fall freely. This hurts too much. My friend's last words before death. This is so hard, but I push myself anyway because what she wanted to tell me was urgent. She died because of it.

I am so sorry, Jess.

You should always know, I had your back no matter what. So, when you got bit, I knew things were going to be hard for you. Early on, I planted a seed within the council, letting them know you were no longer a threat. They believed me because I work for them.

I suck in a sharp breath.

I planned for the worst-case scenarios before we actually met. After you turned, because of the stories that were passed down, they thought you would be the one to destroy their hierarchy, but I had everything put in place to make them let you go. Gosh, Dan is so fucking reckless. He talked about you a lot, and I told him never to bite you. But Dan does whatever the fuck he wants and put you in danger.

I can feel the anger from those words.

I was hired by your family to keep you safe because as much as they wanted to keep you hidden, they weren't able to.

Does she know what happened to my family? Are they still alive?

So I watched you grow up, and I finally approached you when we looked about the same age. I always admired you, Kat, and I had hoped that you'd have the chance to know the real me instead of this persona I had to put up. The life I created became my new life. When we finally met, my whole life got brighter. You were everything to me.

I already know where this is going.

But then you met Theo, and as much as I didn't want you to date him, you were smitten. I tried to tell you he was no good. Always talking in circles and only to make you want him. He was very charismatic, but my gut told me not to trust him.

I wonder if it was because she was close to me and Theo jeopardized our relationship.

At the time I wasn't sure why he was so obsessed with you, but it was like he had to have you.

She clearly hasn't met Ash and Az. *And she never will.*

When I knew there was no way of stopping the relationship from happening because you were so deeply in love with him, I decided to do something more permanent. I didn't want you to harm the people around you because I knew you'd hate yourself and I didn't want people knowing what you were. So I bound you. It was the only way, Kat. I'm so sorry.

I can almost hear her words whispered in my ears. How it saddened her to do this to me.

You're too dangerous now and you'll become a target.

The next words sound off to me.

This was extremely hard information to find. No one knows the information I'm about to tell you, but this concerns you and your family. I did my best, Kat, I truly did, and I hope that after all of this you can forgive me. Maybe in another life we'll find each other again.

I hope so too Jess. There was so much of my life I wanted you to know, and there is so much you still need to tell me.

But enough of that, I have to tell you the reason why I wanted you to see me so urgently. I'm here to tell you how to unbind it, and about the danger you're in, not only from the council but from—

And that's all that it says. There is nothing more. My heart shatters all over again. I turn it over but there's only more splatters of blood. She is not what I thought she was.

I hold the letter to my heart not caring that I have her bloodied letter close to me. My best friend, my rock, she's gone, and I don't know how I'm going to handle this.

A shiny object bounces off my mirror. I get up and walk to my open window, pushing it shut and pulling the blinds down. I'm too tired to care.

Chapter Twenty-seven

Benji

It's Friday, and it's been a little over two weeks since Kat has sought us out. I'm going crazy. My wolf is losing his shit. As her boss, I almost want to demand that she go to work just so I can be near her. Every time she sees me, she runs and hides in her room. Lily has to bring her food up, but she hasn't eaten much. All the progress she's made in gaining weight, and now she's backtracking. She only asks Lily for salad. It's like she's retreating back to her comfort foods, but in her case, her comfort food is nothing delicious and everything healthy...yuck

Her kids are getting worried. They've never seen her this way before. She's a shell of her vibrant self.

So, it's a surprise to see her up and in the kitchen. I look around to see if someone's playing tricks on me. Her kids walk in and halt next to me, one on each side.

She looks so frail, thin, and pale, and I hate myself for giving her so much space. Now that she's out of her room, I'm not letting her go back to her old ways.

"Mom." Ezra hesitates and we're all shocked that she's up and eating at the kitchen table. "Everything okay?" The new norm has been for Kat to be in her room all day. The kids have been the only ones that she allowed in.

I've been trying to see her, but she just kept pushing us aside, telling us that she wasn't ready and that she needed time.

She has dark circles under her eyes as she smiles sadly. "I think it's time I try to get out of my room and get some fresh air."

The kids run up and throw their arms around her, and I can tell they've missed their mom. It hasn't been easy for them either. They're still mourning their old lives, the absence of their father, and now the death of their aunt. They've been staying with their friends a couple of nights a week and it's helped them mourn.

"Do you guys want to hang out today?" Kat asks her kids.

"Mom, we have school." Ava tries to hide the worry in her voice that her mom has really lost her mind.

"I'll call into the school and you guys can come and hang out with me." The kids look at each other and shrug.

"Okay," Ava says in a small voice. "We've missed you." I see the flash of hurt cross Kat's eyes, and I don't think the kids noticed, but I'm sure Kat is thinking about how bad of a mother she is for needing some time to herself.

"Go put your backpacks away." They head out of the kitchen leaving us alone.

"Benji I—" she starts softly, looking down and playing with the hem of her shirt before looking back up at me with her big brown eyes. "I'm sorry I've been ignoring you." She sighs like she's tired. "I've missed you." She bites her bottom lip, my body is vibrating with the need to go to her and pull her lip down so I can kiss it, but instead, I stand there waiting to see what she says next. "Am I fired?" she blurts out.

"What?" I scrunch my brows. "No, of course not. Why would you think that?"

"Because I haven't let the bosses know that I'll be out of work for two weeks."

"You won't ever get fired," I chuckle

"Why is that?" She lifts her brow up.

"We won't ever fire you." She puts her hand on her hips, reminding me that her sass is somewhere in there hiding. There she is. There's my girl.

"Why? Is it because we're dating?"

Yeah, that's part of it, but I don't tell her that because that's not all. "You're a good worker, a quick learner, and you know how to get the job done."

She snorts. "Benji, I've only been working there for two days and have taken a little more than two weeks off."

"And you were wonderful those two days." My smile widens and she snickers.

"I'm playing at the lounge today." I scratch my head nervously. I've never been afraid to ask someone if they wanted to see me play as much as I am now. "Do you want to come by and watch?"

She looks so carefree when she answers. "I'd love that. I knew when I first saw you that you would be in a band."

I come closer to her, placing my palm on her cheek and watching her lean into it. "You were right. We're called The Misfit Kings."

"I like the name." She looks like she wants to ask a question but hesitates. "What is it, Kitty Kat?"

"Can I borrow your car so I can take my kids out?" she asks.

"Of course," I tell her, reaching into my back pocket and pulling my keys out.

She grabs them and gives me a whisper of a kiss. "Thank you."

She pulls away too soon, way too soon. "You're welcome."

The kids come back downstairs, excited to be hanging out with their mom. "I'll bring it back in one piece." She winks and heads out the kitchen door that leads outside.

I stare at the door for a long moment wondering if I imagined this whole scenario. "Was that Kat?" Ash walks into the room grabbing a cup from the cabinet and pouring himself some coffee.

"Yep."

"Is she doing any better?" I see it in his eyes that he hates not being able to see Kat. No matter how much he says he doesn't like her, I know he actually cares for her on some level. Plus, there's no denying the pull we have toward her.

"I think we'll actually get to see her more often now."

"Good. We need our best worker back." I roll my eyes at his big lie.

"I'm going to practice with the guys. Kat says she's coming to see me tonight." I know I can't hide my excitement. It's just been way too long since I got to hang out with her.

Ash looks at me with wide eyes. "Really?" he says in disbelief.

"Yeah. Any news on the best friend?"

“I think we may have found Jess’ body.” Now it’s my turn to look shocked. “I’m going to have to go check it out. I think it’ll provide some closure for Kat to give her friend a proper burial.

“Alright brother, let me know if you guys need any help, I’ll be at the lounge.”

“Hey man.” Drake hands me my standup bass. It’s a few minutes before we start playing, and I’m looking out into the crowd searching for my girl. “I can’t wait to meet her. Your lyrics have been on point lately, and I want to meet the girl behind your inspiration,” he says as he grabs his guitar from the side of the stage.

“Yeah, man, we’ve been getting a lot of views on YouTube and women are going wild for those lyrics. They think you’re singing to them.” Steve chuckles from behind me, messing with the drums.

“Yo, that girl with violet hair is smokin’.” Steve whistles as I adjust the tuning knobs.

“Oh, hell yeah she is,” Drake says, coming closer to me. “I think I’m going to talk to her.”

“Not if I get to her first,” Steve says, playing with the drums. “I’m just glad Benji already has a girl or else it’d be more competition, now I don’t have to fight with him too.”

"I'm going to be the one that takes her home," Steve says with so much confidence. "She's looking at me."

"No. She's looking at me," Drake responds.

"You know women fall for the drummer, it's a fact." Both of these guys are lucky I'm no longer on the market.

"Is that—" Steve pauses next to me. "A heart tattoo in the corner of her eye?" My stare shoots up, landing on light brown eyes.

"None of you fuckers are getting her. That's Kat."

"Well fuck," Drake says with disappointment.

"Well, there goes my plan." Steve comes closer to us. "You're one lucky man." He pats my shoulder before he leaves and sits behind his drums.

I get off the stage, with a big grin on my face. "You came." I look at her hair. "And you changed your hair. You look beautiful, Kat." It's a deep violet that makes her eyes pop.

She touches her hair. "Thank you." Her voice is small like she's self-conscious about it. "I needed a change."

"Well, you look perfect." I lean in to kiss her when someone clears their throat, preventing me from going all the way to her lips. She grins, taking my breath away.

I look behind me at my friends crossing their arms. "Are you going to introduce us?"

"Kat, this is Drake, he plays the guitar and Steve plays the drums."

They get closer to her, and my hand stiffens and forms a fist. Kat grabs it with her soft hands, helping me calm down. When it comes to her and her kids, I tend to not think straight. As an Alpha, I can't let myself lose control. We already have Az.

"Very nice to meet you guys," she says in a cool voice, but I can hear how strained it is. She may look composed on the outside but she's anything but.

Tyler comes up behind her, wrapping an arm around her waist. "Let's go grab a drink and let Benji get back on stage. I think people are waiting for him."

I look around and find everyone staring at us. Now that Kat is out of the house all I want to do is be with her. I want to bring her on stage, I open my mouth to tell her but Tyler cuts me off. "Go, Benji, I'll be here with her." He starts pulling her away. "Come on, Kat, let's go to the bar." I watch her until she's out of sight then I walk back to the stage.

"You guys ready?" I turn to face my friends and they both nod their heads.

The whole time my eyes are glued to Kat. They don't wander from her beautiful face. I'm almost afraid she's going to disappear again.

She smiles up at me while I sing my heart out for her. She sways her hips side to side while Tyler and Ash are both on each side of her.

Az is here somewhere, I can feel his eyes, but they're not on me. I know he's watching Kat, and I know she feels it because every so often, she glances away from me to a dark corner of the club like she knows exactly where he is. Whatever they did in his room, they formed an attachment to each other. He hasn't brought another woman home or even tried seeking one out. He's just as smitten as Tyler and me. It's only a matter of time before Ash can't resist her anymore.

Once the set is done, I rush from the stage and lift her up, kissing her with so much force that she gasps. The crowd cheers, but I don't pay attention to anyone but her.

Chapter Twenty-eight

Kat

The next day, I'm not feeling myself completely, but I've accepted the fact that my best friend is gone. It hasn't been easy to admit that she won't be with me again. This hurts more than when Theo told me he didn't want to be with me. Actually, there's no comparison.

It was so damn hard not to tell Ash to take me back to the brothel. I think that's why I avoided him the most, and although Az helped me with my pain, I've been too scared to go back.

Yesterday I spent the day with my kids, granted we couldn't go outside of the property, but it was still nice. We had lunch and went out to a beautiful lake that's located on the property.

After Ava went to work and Ezra went to his room, I went to get my hair done. I wanted a change. Everything else has changed, why not my hair?

My kids were so shocked. I chuckle when I remember their open mouths and wide eyes. "The color suits you," Ava had said.

Ash's cigarette fell from his lips when he saw me, and I took that as a good sign. Az has yet to show his face, but I could feel him following me through the halls and at the lounge. I briefly wonder if he's hurt that I ignored him for more than two weeks, especially because we had a very intimate moment, but I needed time to myself.

Now I need to get back to my normal routine. I told Benji last night that I was ready to get back to work at the Crescent Lounge.

Truthfully, I was a little afraid about going back there because that's where I was being watched by Dan and was abducted a block from there. I put on a brave face yesterday, but I think the only way to normalize it is to face it.

It's Saturday night, and though I'm not supposed to work today, the Crescent Lounge is understaffed and they need my help.

“Do you really have to go in?” Benji stands by the door watching me as I put on a deep shade of purple lipstick. “Can’t we hang out?” he pouts.

“Benji, I haven’t worked in more than two weeks. It’s the weekend and it’ll be extremely busy. The people there will need help.”

He sighs dramatically laying across my bed. “Must you dress like that?” He waves his arms up and down. “I won’t be able to keep my hands to myself,” he groans, rubbing his face.

I stand up checking on the knee length boots and black skirt I’m wearing. Maybe I should wear something more modest. Nah, fuck anyone who doesn’t like my outfit.

“Fuck, those boots, Kat. I have a hard on now.” I giggle and shake my head.

“Alright guys let’s go,” Tyler shouts from the door, but his mouth hangs open when he sees me.

“Umm...Benj—”

“I know,” he cuts in. “She’s killing us.” I laugh as we start walking out of my room.

“Oh shoot. I forgot my dagger. I’ll meet you guys there.” They nod their heads and keep walking. I go back to my room and grab it from my drawer and get my belt that ties around my thigh. I put it on then secure my weapon. I go to the mirror, checking to see if you can see it, but it’s completely hidden.

I attempt to close my blinds but something shiny catches my eye. I look out the window, but the glint is gone. It's not the first time I've seen some sort of light out there, but it's probably just headlights in the distance.

"We should probably mention it to the guys tonight. It could be nothing but better to be safe than sorry. I'm not trying to get kidnapped again." My wolf narrows her eyes before we walk out.

I walk down to the other side of the hall and knock on Ezra's door. Nothing. I knock harder. Nothing. Fuck Ezra. I turn the knob but it's locked. I grab my phone and call him. "Hey, Mom!" He sounds chipper. "Where the hell are you?" He opens the door to his room and hangs up. "You should have knocked."

"I did. Three times."

"Oh sorry," he says, taking off his headphones. "I was playing a game." He turns back to the enormous computer screens that weren't there before.

"How'd you get that in here?"

"Oh, that was Tyler. He gave them to me." Of course he did. He's got two big gaming screens with a chair that looks way too comfortable.

"Okay, well, if you need anything just call." He puts on his headphones before giving me two thumbs up and closing the door.

"Hey Ava." I knock on her door before she opens it, looking sickly. "What the hell happened to you?"

"I just got my period."

"Lies." My wolf shouts in my head. We can't smell it on her.

"What is it really, Ava?" I cross my arms, hopefully showing her that she can talk to me about anything.

"Don't you have to go to work?" she says tiredly.

"No, and if you're feeling sick then I should stay." There's no negotiating that.

"We've been through so much shit. I'm just tired." She closes her eyes.

"I'll get you a therapist." I'm not sure why I didn't think about this earlier.

"I don't want or need a therapist. I promise, if I feel worse, I'll call you. I have a lot of homework to do."

"Fine. I'll have my phone with me." Thankfully this skirt has pockets.

I start walking. "Mom," I look back, "You look hot." She smiles weakly and closes the door.

The club is busy and full of people today. Tyler and I are working behind the bar, and I haven't had a moment to myself. Benji is in the VIP area. There's a DJ tonight, and every once in a while, I catch myself dancing.

By the end of the night my feet are hurting and I'm ready for bed. "How are you feeling Kat?" Tyler asks as we are wiping down the counters. All the party goers are gone and it's only the employees that linger.

"Fucking tired."

"Yeah, I feel that," he says as he sprays another table and continues to wipe it down. "So I didn't get a chance to ask you, but I wanted to see if you need to talk about the kills?" I stop what I'm doing to stare at him. "You killed two people and then witnessed your friend..."

He doesn't want to finish the sentence, so I answer him, saving him from saying it. "I'm actually surprised that I haven't thought about the kills." I thought I would feel guilty by not thinking about it, but surprisingly I don't. "Maybe my wolf part keeps me sane." He nods like he understands where I'm coming from. "Ava is a different story though." He stops what he's doing and comes close to me.

"What do you mean?"

"She's been looking paler than usual. I think all of this might be getting to her. I think Ezra might be using video games as an escape. Which is fine. I also saw that setup you got him." He smiles sheepishly, "It's fine, I'm not mad. I'm glad he has something to distract him from the real world. I suggested a therapist to Ava, but she wasn't interested. Maybe I should buy her some books, at least for now."

"Yeah, I think that would be perfect. We have a bookstore in our shopping center."

“I saw it. We didn’t go in, but I want to go see what they have.” Books are life, I’m sure Ava will enjoy reading to take her mind off the real world.

“How about what happened to Jess?” He crosses his arms leaning on one of the tables.

“That’s still a wound that hurts. I hate that I wasn’t there for her and you guys didn’t get to meet her. She would have loved all four of you.”

“Well, we’re a much better upgrade from your ex.” I laugh and we go back to cleaning. “Oh hey, I almost forgot. So, two weeks ago I saw something in the distance just outside of my window. It was shining. I didn’t think anything of it until I saw it again tonight. It might not be anything but figured I’d let you know.”

His body stills for a moment like he’s trying to figure something out. “I’ll check the cameras tonight and see if I can find anything.”

His shoulders stiffen and his eyes avoid mine. They’re definitely keeping something from me.

Chapter Twenty-nine

Ash

"We thought we found it, but the body wasn't there," Az tells me as we sit outside sitting side-by-side on outdoor patio chairs. "We have no idea what supernatural she was, and Kat didn't even know she was a supernatural."

I twirl the cigarette in one hand, putting it behind my ear, and swish the brandy around my glass with the other. "So, the next best thing is to give Jess a proper funeral. We may not know where her body is, but we could give Katarina this one thing."

"Some supernaturals dissolve into thin air, so that might have been a possibility."

"Do you have any theories on who might have killed her?" I stare out at the crackling fire pit.

“I have my suspicions.” He stands up and tucks both hands in his pockets, deep in thought.

I lean in closer from my chair. “Well, share them.”

Az sighs like he’s exhausted, and I know we can all relate to that. Katarina being locked away for two weeks put us all on edge. “I think it’s the witch.”

“What!” I shout, nearly spitting out my drink.

Az leans on the wall. “Yeah, it doesn’t make any sense. Maybe Dante was lying and he did kill her.”

“No. He looked as shocked as Kat. I’m positive he didn’t do it.” I rub my temples. “Well, Katarina needs a funeral for her friend. I think it would help her with the grieving process.”

“Even if we have nobody?” Az questions.

“Yeah, I think we should explain to her that when some supernaturals die, they just vanish.” Her human side expects her to have a human funeral, so that’s what we’ll do. I think if we set something up with her for tomorrow, it’ll help her let go. I’ll have the betas make proper arrangements and we can have a funeral tomorrow evening.

Katarina looks gorgeous with her black dress and violet hair. She’s wearing sunglasses, but I assume her eyes are purple behind those dark shades.

I walk up to Katarina, and Ava looks back at both of us. She’s been wearing a lot of heavy makeup lately. I think it's to hide the puffiness from crying over her aunt. "Mom, you and Ash match," I'm assuming it's because we are both wearing black but so is everyone else. "You make a cute couple." I don't need to see her eyes, but her cheeks are scarlet red.

Before Katarina opens her mouth, Ava says, "Gotta go," and walks over to her friends.

"I guess we do match." She looks even more stunning up close.

We huddle around a clearing where we got a bench that says, "In loving memory of Jess." Katarina cries softly when we show her.

Tyler and Benji each hold her hand while Az sticks to the shadows and I overlook the area, making sure there are no threats lurking. Ever since Dan got in, I've been more careful, even around our own property. Strange smells have been showing up, and I can't seem to pinpoint where they're coming from. Not to mention, Tyler's cameras look like they're recording live when they're not, he only found out when Katarina mentioned some sort of light out her window. Someone is messing with our property, and we have an inkling feeling it's her. I have my enforcers and betas patrolling the property twenty-four seven.

All the betas showed up along with families in the community. They all keep their distance but are there to show support. I couldn't be prouder of my pack.

The whole ceremony was beautiful. We got a human priest and we all pretended we were normal. Although, I think he could sense there was something quite different about us. Once he was done, he couldn't get out of here fast enough.

The crowd leaves and only the five of us are left. We wait for a very long time until Katarina tells us she's ready to go.

She breathes easier, but I know that she'll want time for herself, and so we all give her the space she needs while keeping an eye on her. Hopefully, it won't take another two weeks of solitude. The guys really missed her.

"And you." My wolf makes sure I don't forget.

"Okay maybe a little for me too."

Chapter Thirty

Tyler

It's noon the next day and I still haven't seen Kat. I almost leave my room wanting to knock on Kat's door. The urge is so strong I nearly do it, but then remember she'll seek one of us when she's ready. I'm not the jealous type, far from it, but I was shocked the day she went to Az's room two and half weeks ago for comfort instead of mine.

Benji left for the Crescent Lounge since he and his band are playing tonight, while I grabbed a pair of headphones in an effort to distract myself from barging into Kat's room. Putting on Dre, I kick back on my bed and try to relax. There's something about old Rap I can't seem to get enough of.

I'm blasting the music loud. I'll be surprised if my eardrums work after this.

My phone lights up with a message from Ash. I grab it from my desk.

Ash: Let's talk in the kitchen

It's our group message, so we all got the same text. I take off my headphones and rest them around my neck, feeling the vibrations. I walk out the door and I can no longer help it. I walk into her room and she's sound asleep. I close the door making a quiet click sound and head downstairs.

Ash and Az are already there. "I bought burritos," Az says, pulling one from the bag and handing it to me. I sit in one of the chairs while Az sits across from me.

"Lily left?" I ask, expecting her to be here somewhere.

"Yeah, I told her to go home. Figured she was going to go pry and ask Katarina a million questions before she was ready to answer to them." Ash says standing up across from me and already eating. Probably a good idea. I love Lily, but she's nosey as fuck.

"Does anyone know if Kat's eaten yet?" Az asks.

"She hasn't," Ash says with certainty, and I'm wondering if he's been keeping a close eye in her room.

“How is she doing?” Benji walks into the kitchen already going for the bag of food. He sits down next to me.

“I checked on her before I came here but she was asleep,” I say through a mouthful of food.

“I don’t think the funeral helped, she’s still in her room.” Az says, already cleaning up his area. He inhaled his food. He once told us that he always ate fast because he grew up poor and hardly had anything to eat, and when he did have food, he’d have to eat so fast before one of the older kids tried to take it away from him.

“Give it time, Az. She’ll come out soon.” Benji glares daggers at him and I chuckle. He’s still sour that Kat went to see Az instead of him.

“We haven’t talked about what Silas wants with Ava.” This has me a little on edge too.

“I have no fucking clue, but we have to be wary,” Ash says, taking another bite. “I don’t trust those fuckers, and I don’t trust Katarina.” I almost blurt out *liar.* His act about not caring is getting old.

“She went out of her way to get me the medicine,” Benji adds, clenching his jaw. “If she wanted to kill us, don’t you think she would have let me die?” Benji’s eyes change color, and the smell of violence assaults the air.

“Calm down, Benji” Ash rolls his eyes like he doesn’t see Benji already on edge. “I said we are going to protect her.” He likes to act like he’s the leader of this group, but he's honestly not. I don't mind it, and neither do the other guys, but even if he didn't want any of us to protect Kat, I'd remind him of the way I beat the shit out of his ass when we were brawling not so long ago.

Benji's eyes go back to normal. "I really fucking hate how the witch took our powers. We can't communicate the way we used to."

"There are always cell phones." I give Benji a pointed look.

"Not reliable, they can easily be hacked." I look at Ash because I know what he did to find Kat. He purposely ignores the glare I'm throwing his way and goes back to his food.

"Well, are you going to tell us what happened?" Az plays with his knife like he doesn't have a care in the world. But the way his shoulders tense says otherwise.

He sighs as if he knows what he's going to tell us will ruin his appetite. "I already told you guys, we found Jess, Katarina's best friend dead, but what I didn't tell you three is that I also found Dante." He doesn't get to finish before we all start shouting at once.

"How does this keep happening and why are you telling us just now?" Az asks, leaning forward and pulling his knife from his pocket.

"I should have killed him when I had the chance," Benji growls.

Even I'm surprised. "He's one lucky son of a bitch." I shout with the rest of them. "Why didn't you kill him? It's within our rights."

He closes his eyes and rubs them before pushing the empty plate away from him. "I wanted to murder him, but I needed to get Katarina out of there." What he doesn't say is that she was more important. I can see it in his eyes, but he just won't give in. "The killer was nearby, and I had a weeping Katarina on the floor. There was no time to do anything else." We all nod in understanding. "There is something else, I haven't told you guys because I'm trying to figure this out myself. When I caught up to Katarina, she did something to—" he suddenly stops, that delicious scent wafting into the kitchen before she even steps foot. It's so sweet and tangy. I look at my brothers and they also look to be straining.

We're in fucking trouble now.

Chapter Thirty-one

Kat

Throughout the night, my bedroom door opens and closes quietly as people check on me, but I'm too exhausted to open my eyes. My kids came in giving me a kiss and telling me they love me before they left, but my body was too exhausted to respond.

The guys gave me a beautiful memorial for Jess, and I was finally able to say goodbye to her. Though I know I was meant to feel closure, all I can feel is the need to avenge her death.

Whoever killed her will pay.

I think we've all grown closer since her death. It has made me realize I need to cherish the people in my life, and that means Ash and Az as well, even if they both drive me nuts.

My stomach growls, reminding me I haven't eaten in a while, and I get a sudden craving for chocolate cake. I get up from the bed knowing that Lily has probably made some type of dessert. I'm really hoping for the gooey kind like brownies. I walk down the stairs to the kitchen. I'm not even ashamed about skipping breakfast or lunch or whatever the fuck time it is. I'm too raw that my mind forgets to nag me about eating.

When I come downstairs, I expect them to all breathe a sigh of relief to see me out of my room and ready to go, but instead, when I walk in, everyone immediately stops what they're doing and stares at me. Oh...kay... This is weird. Something in the air has shifted.

Benji and Tyler are seated at the bar next to each other. Ash is leaning against the fridge in silence, and Az is twirling a knife, leaning against the bar trying to look relaxed, but the slight twitch in the corner of his eye says otherwise.

Why are they all staring at me like I'm a snack they want to devour? Perhaps if it were only Tyler and Benji, I could understand, but I'm not used to seeing anything but hate in Az or Ash's eyes. Maybe Az has changed his mind after our encounter a few weeks ago, but I've been keeping my distance from him, unsure of what our night meant to him. I don't think he's angry at me anymore, but I do think I might have hurt Az since I haven't sought him out.

My wolf is jumping up and down with excitement at their heated stares. Her being this giddy makes me twitchy. Something else is going on, something I'm not picking up on.

Their eye colors change, practically glowing, and I want to say something, but all of a sudden, my mouth is parched. I lick my lips and walk into the kitchen, carefully avoiding Az. I can feel the heat radiating off of him even though we're standing five feet apart. I go to the cabinet and open it. Everything in this kitchen is so quiet except for me.

Bringing the glass to the fridge, I grab the cool water pitcher, keeping my eyes on Az the entire time. The only sound in the room right now is the liquid hitting the glass.

I tip the cup to my mouth as they watch my every movement. Ash hands me a burrito and I take a couple of bites while still watching them closely.

"What the fuck is going on, wolf? You better start talking, now!" I shout as I smell their arousals. My heart starts beating faster, responding to their scent. I try to calm it down with deep breaths.

She doesn't get to say anything when there's a deep low growl coming from Ash's stomach. It's so low but demanding, I look his way. We're standing way too close to each other, and my mind runs rampant through the cloudy images of our night at the brothel. It's like I can feel his hands on my bare skin and his lips moving along my collarbone as I stare into his eyes. I take a step back to put some distance between us. We haven't talked about that night, and a part of me thought he was too drunk and high to remember the words he hissed into my ear with his hand wrapped around my throat.

There's a bead of sweat that runs down his brow. It's like he's trying not to lose control, and I know without a doubt, he remembers everything. "Katarina." His voice is strained and it's a long while before he starts speaking again. "When was the last time you had your cycle?" I'm stunned by his question, especially coming from the only one of them I haven't been intimate with. This question is not what I was expecting. I swallow the last bite.

"They're not vampires so they won't try to eat me, right?" I ask my wolf, but she stays silent, providing no help.

I think about it for a second. "Almost a month ago."

"I believe this is her last human period before she goes on a female wolf's cycle," Benji says, barely restraining himself on the chair. His face is turning bright red trying to stay put.

"Oh, you bitch." I snarl at her. *"Why didn't you say anything before?"* My wolf cackles.

“How long is a female wolf’s period?” This is going to suck if it’s more than my six days. I’m going to be so pissed off.

“They range from six to nine months. It depends on the female.” I gape, and he clears his throat. “I mean you get them every six to nine months, not that you’ll have it for that long. They last about five to seven days.” His cheeks turn slightly pink. Tyler looks so adorable.

“No fucking way!” I shout. “You mean I only have to deal with my period maybe twice a year? This is the best news ever!” My smile widens. No more having to deal with it every month and feeling tired and cranky and craving sweets. Oh, and cramps, how could I forget about those? It’s like I summon it when my uterus contracts and I start to feel pain.

“Kat.” Tyler’s breaths are heavy and I almost worry. “So...” he chuckles nervously before starting back up again. “When a female gets their period...” He doesn’t get to finish because Ash finishes it for him.

“We want to fuck.” My face shoots up, his words from that night at the brothel coming to mind again.

“When I take you, I want you to remember every vivid detail of what it’s like to have me fuck you—because I won’t be able to forget it or walk away like it didn’t fucking happen.”

Well, shit. This was the reason for the heated stares. I’m more aware of their bodies now than when I first came in. Benji is holding onto the counter, and his knuckles are turning white by how hard he's gripping it. Tyler is breathing heavily, trying to take calming breaths. Az has his knife's blade pressed into his palm, blood trailing down his arm, as if the pain grounds him. Ash has moved closer than he was before, his pupils dilated. I swallow again, feeling thirsty.

"What do we do now?" I ask my wolf.

"We fuck all of them," she says, and I can almost see her licking her lips, eyeing every single one of them.

"Whatever you do, don't run Katarina," Ash says huskily trying to regain his composure. He pulls out a cigarette from who knows where and lights it up. I've never seen him light one inside the house before. I mean it's not like I've known him for a long time, but the house never smelled like smoke before. "If you run, we won't be able to keep our wolves at bay. They will chase you down and fuck you."

Why does that sound like something I want to do? I know that I shouldn't, but I've always been worked up on my period. Ash's wolf watches me closely as if he knows what I'm thinking, and he growls loudly. "Everyone but Kat, get the fuck out of here."

"I'm not leaving my Kitty Kat with you," Benji voices as Az immediately leaves without a fight.

I can see the venom in Ash's stare, and before he says anything that he'll regret, I jump in. "It's alright." I look at both Benji and Tyler.

"Are you sure, Kat?" Tyler asks, watching for any signs of distress.

"Who the fuck do you think I am?" Ash snaps. "You guys know me better than anyone. You know I wouldn't do anything Katarina doesn't want." He's on edge and I can feel it. Violence mixed with lust.

I smile reassuringly. "I'll be fine." Ash has more restraint than the others give him credit for, maybe even more than me. But the way Ash grabs another cigarette and starts smoking it, I notice the slight tremble in his hand.

The others stand still, violence brewing in all three sets of eyes before me. "I said get the fuck out." Ash's voice booms through the kitchen, and the other men go rigid. They'd fight for me if I wanted them to, but I really need this moment with Ash.

They both look at me once more before they head outside through the kitchen door. Once the door closes softly, I turn to Ash.

The way he stares at me is like nothing that I've felt before. I've never seen him like this, his mind so clouded with want and need.

"If I stay, will you regret what happens?" I ask. I need to be sure that he won't hate himself for this.

As for me, I've already made up my mind and know what I want.

He tilts his head, staring at me through his wolf's eyes. Nothing about this interaction is human. "No." That's all I need, that one word.

I give him a wicked smile before turning on my heels and sprinting out of the kitchen and up the stairs. I'm panting and it has nothing to do with me being tired, more of wanting him to get me. This game we're playing stirs up my wolf too.

She's been wanting him for a long time, and I know he's been wanting me too, even if he tries to hide it.

I can hear his footsteps right behind me. He makes no effort to stay quiet. I go down the hall and open a door to the closet.

My heartbeat pumps erratically as I will myself to calm down. I'm not sure what's going to happen when he finds me, but I know I can't wait.

I ignore the pain in my belly for now. I really hate having my period.

It starts to get quiet, and I make sure to keep my mouth shut. "Where are you, Katarina?" His footsteps are getting closer. My body shakes from excitement instead of fear.

I hear him opening the doors to other rooms as he looks for me. I bite my thumb nail trying to stay quiet. "Once I find you, you're mine." Those are the sweetest words he's ever said to me. All I want is for him to find me, but I won't make this easy on him.

When he opens another door, I quickly open mine and sprint down the hall to another set of stairs, and I go up them, trying to open a door, but it's locked. Shit, I can hear him coming after me. I try to open the one next to it and nothing. Shit, shit, shit.

I look across the hall, trying my luck on the other side. I twist the handle and it opens and I immediately close it and lock it. I can hear him trying the first two doors that I tried. He won't be able to open this one either and he'll think I'm not here.

"Oh, I love a challenge, Katarina," I slightly tremble at his words, still grinning. I hear him pounding on the first door. He manages to get it open, and I debate whether to leave this one and go down the stairs but decide against it. He would hear my footsteps and I'd get caught.

I hear him shuffling through whatever is behind that door before he closes it and moves to the next one. I look around this room trying to figure out where to hide. This room is a lot smaller than mine.

I decide to hide in a small corner behind a drawer next to the closet. I doubt he'd notice a space this tiny.

I squeeze my body in there right before the door slams open.

Chapter Thirty-two

Ash

She's in here. I know she is. Her sweet scent is in every corner of this room. She thinks she can hide from me, but she has nowhere to go that I won't be able to find her. I love the challenge of chasing her down. Her arousal is thick and I'm drowning in it.

I can't wait to be in between her legs. This lust is making me crazy. I check underneath the bed and growl in frustration when she's not there.

Standing back up, I immediately go to the closet, opening it wide, thinking that I have her.

"Katarina, you're not getting away from me." My voice barely sounds human. "If you show yourself,

I'll go easy on you." That won't really happen, they're just sweet words to lure her out.

I wait a few more moments sitting on the bed, my ears perking up, paying attention to a noise as I look around the bedroom. She has to be here somewhere. That's when I notice a small gap that almost no one could fit into...unless you're as small as Katarina.

"Have it your way," I gloat, excited to have found my prize. I walk toward her hiding spot silently, knowing that she'll be there. I lower my body and say, "I found you, Katarina." She lets out a small yelp, clearly surprised at being caught. I was too quiet for her.

Her arousal mixed with her cycle surrounds me, and I don't think I can wait any longer.

She climbs out of the small space and I take in her body. She steps toward me hesitantly, and I lick my lips, wanting her mouth on mine, but I wait patiently as she comes to me.

"Are you sure?" she asks, looking deep into my eyes trying to confirm that this is really what I want.

Instead of answering, I move quickly, grabbing her and pinning her to the bed. As much as I want to take her to my bed and see her spread out, I don't think I can wait anymore.

I walked away from her once, I'll be damned if I do it twice.

She faces me with excitement and a slight hint of fear in her gaze. I look down at her body as she's gripping on to her leggings. She glances down to see what I'm looking at. "I've never had sex on my period." Her cheeks turn pink.

I push her hair from her face. "If you're uncomfortable—"

"No! I want this," she says, cutting me off. She bites her lip hard, and I know something else is bothering her. "Should we maybe grab a towel to put under me?"

"No," I growl. I pull down on her chin with my thumb and she lets it go. I lean down and claim her mouth the way I did the first time we met. The taste of sweet cherries mixed with the vanilla scent of tobacco creates the most perfect blend.

I want her naked and underneath me, wanting to feel that soft skin. All I've been trying to do is keep my hands to myself, but I don't think I can let her go again. We pull apart and I grab her shirt, pulling off her clothes.

She's not wearing a bra, so as soon as I take her shirt off, her tits bounce. I knead her breasts, loving how they fit in my hands. She moans quietly, but when I look up, I see that flame has been ignited. She wants me as much as I want her, and for some odd reason, that brings me comfort.

I take a step back to remove her pants when she puts one hand on her waistband for a brief second before letting go. Not wanting to waste any more time, I grab her underwear and pants and throw them off to the side.

Her heartbeat pounds faster and faster as she lays exactly how I envisioned her. Naked underneath me.

Her eyes watch my every movement as I undo my tie and undress quickly. Leaving only my boxers, I climb back on top of her while she lays completely bare.

I know that she's wet enough that I won't hurt her, but there's worry behind her eyes, and I want to make her feel at ease.

Sure, I'm impatient, but I don't want our first time to be meaningless.

I want to thrust my fingers inside of her, but I also don't want to make her squirm. She's going to have to get used to it because once she's on it again, I'm sure all of us will try to fight each other to be near her.

I was actually pretty impressed that my brothers let me have her. I know that they're pissed I made them leave, but I can't control it. I need her. I need to be inside of her.

I get close to her belly and inhale her smell, closing my eyes and taking it in. I know she doesn't consider this normal, but as a shifter, it's what we do. This is the time we want to be with our mate. *Mate?* That ship sailed a long time ago.

I take her hardened peak in my mouth, biting it gently with my canines. She gasps but pushes them out wanting more. I trail soft kisses down her bare stomach going all the way down to the inside of her thighs. She inhales sharply when I'm closer to her core.

I line my cock on her entrance and dive right into her slick pussy. She fists the sheets and moans. I thrust inside her, loving how she completely lets go. I know she's enjoying it. I'm assuming she's never had sex while she was on her cycle.

"You know," she pants. "I've always been my horniest when I was on my period, but I was afraid to act on it," she says, confirming my suspicions.

"You never have to worry about being afraid of your needs." I bring my mouth down to hers, no longer kissing her softly but more demanding. "You're mine, Katarina." My voice is harsh and possessive, startling me. This moment is too raw for both of us. I think that's why my body wants to claim her as ours. I want her to know she belongs to me.

Her violet eyes light up. I'm becoming more accustomed to seeing her like this. She's special.

My dick starts to expand letting me know my release is coming soon. I pound harder, faster, watching her tits bounce with every thrust, I give them a small slap and watch as her lips part in pure bliss.

"Damn this feels too good. I don't want this to end." My cock starts to swell up and something very unexpected happens, something that shouldn't have happened, but I'm riding the wave so hard I can't stop myself, even if I wanted to. I just let our bodies do what they've been wanting to do. A knot forms inside of her, keeping my dick from leaving her sweet cunt. Even if I want to pull out, it's too late, there is nothing more I can do.

"This feels so right, Ash," she cries out, and I know exactly what she means even if there's a nagging feeling telling me that what we're doing shouldn't have been possible.

I bring my lips crashing down to hers. We explore each other by biting, nipping. My cock keeps pounding into her and her groans get louder. I silence them by bruising her lips with mine. I go down to her chest as my dick thrusts on its own without me needing to move my hips. She scratches my back while I bite down on her nipple, drawing a small amount of blood. She gasps in surprise.

She clenches harder, squeezing me so tightly while she comes. Soon after, she's pumping me while I come inside of her, my jizz making her orgasm again. Finally, the knot loosens up and I manage to pull out.

Panting, I lay my body next to hers. She sits up on her elbows and gasps at the mess in between her legs. There's blood all over the sheets, on my dick, on her legs. She tries to get up, but I immediately lay my hand on her stomach.

"I should clean up," she says in a small voice. I turn to her reddened cheeks and get mad when I notice the embarrassment she has on her face. She shouldn't be self-conscious; this is completely normal.

"Leave it," I say, rubbing her stomach.

"But it's all over."

"We'll clean it later." One minute I'm staring at her and the next I'm on top of her again, losing control and grabbing her by the neck, squeezing it hard. She pulls at my arms trying to claw her way out of my hold. Her face is starting to turn purple. She's wheezing, but I hold on tightly suffocating her.

Chapter Thirty-three

Kat

Something is very wrong.

We went from having amazing sex to him trying to choke the living shit out of me, and not the kinky kind. I'm starting to see black spots, and I know if I pass out, he'll surely kill me.

He looks crazed, on a mission to end my life. This is not him at all. I try to talk to him and let him know, but it's no use. I can't spit a single word and the guys left the house to give us space. There is no one to hear me struggling or to help me out.

My vision changes. I'm losing this fight. I'm terrified. This can't be happening to me. Tears stream from the corners of my eyes. All I want to do is scream, but I can't do that either.

I try to reach his neck, but it's no use. He's way stronger than me. Still, I try to hold onto anything I can, reaching for his face to do something to impair his vision, but he's too far for my arms. My body starts to tremble, my lungs burn, I want to cough so badly but can't.

"Stop!" I try to tell him, but he's squeezing tight on my vocal cords.

Using my legs, I move them up and kick his balls a couple of times until he goes down. Sudden strength consumes my body, this resembles the same night I bested him when he tried to stuff me into the car and take me home from Jess' house. It seems like it only comes when my emotions are heightened.

He gets off me and I quickly get out of the bed, touching my neck, which now feels tender. "Ash." My voice is hoarse. "Stand down," I wheeze out.

He seems to snap from whatever happened. "Oh my God, Katarina, are you okay?" He tries to step close, but I take a long step back. "I am so sorry. I didn't mean to do that." His voice breaks and it's there in his eyes, the regret of what he did.

I watch him warily while I pick up my clothes from the floor. I don't completely trust him. He did try to kill me.

"Now you know the last part of the curse. I can't say it out loud, but you saw what it did to me." He lowers his shoulders looking exhausted, and I feel for him, but I have to make sure he won't try to murder me again.

"The witch controls you." He only nods his head.

"My brothers," he gasps. "I have to check on them."

I sprint to the bathroom in my room to clean up and find period panties in one of the drawers. I don't know who thought of stocking these, but I'm forever grateful. I get dressed quickly and go to walk down the stairs when the whole house shakes and I'm thrown on the floor. Ash shows up, trying to pick me up, but I hold my hand watching him warily. I'm still shaken about what happened. My throat is sore and my voice is still raspy. In the back of my mind, I also know that something occurred between us, something that wasn't supposed to happen.

I swallow hard and wince in pain, I look anywhere else but him. From the corner of my eyes there's a flash of hurt that crosses his face, but it's gone before I can decipher if it was really there. He pulls back, grabbing his phone instead. "What the fuck is going on, Tyler?"

I can't hear his response because a loud boom rocks the house. We make our way down the stairs as I eye them warily. I have a feeling it's going to go off again when I'm going down and I'll end up rolling to the bottom.

As I'm debating how best to descend the stairs without falling, another one hits the house. "Nope. Not happening." I throw my arms out for balance and walk back up the stairs.

Ash growls, tossing me over his shoulder and rushing down the stairs. My body tenses, but he doesn't show signs of being possessed, so I relax against him, but only slightly, still keeping a close eye on him.

He's a lot more graceful than I am. We make it down with no problem even while being tossed around.

His phone rings again and he picks up. My hand is on the handle of the door, ready to face whatever bombs are out there. "Don't op—" he starts, but I swing the door open and stare out into the forest.

Mouth gaped wide open. "Oh, fuck. It's Krissy. What the fuck is she doing here? Does she want to take these men away from me too?" I say quietly, more to myself. Is that the whole reason she wanted to meet, to see if I'd found another man? Little does she know, I have four. I smirk.

"Focus, Kat." My wolf brings me out of my haze. *"There is so much more going on that you're not seeing."*

Another explosion rocks me, and I flinch, the noise is way louder out here. I look over to find Benji. He's the one that's causing the whole house to shake.

He looks strange, his eyes are glazed over the same way Ash's were, I nearly run to him but hesitate, my hands going back up to my throat. I'm not looking for a repeat.

Tyler and Az come running from behind the house. Their faces are pale as if they've just seen a ghost. My body shivers thinking I'm going to see a spirit. I'm not ready for that kind of supernatural yet.

I open my mouth but shut it when Ash speaks. "Krissy—" Huh? Does he know her? That's when all the pieces start falling into place.

"It's nice to see you again." Ash smiles but it looks anything but friendly. I almost take a step back by the violence in his voice.

"Oh, Kat." She peers straight at me with a crazed look and my body slightly cowers. "I'm glad you came out of that hole." She looks behind me to the house and I want to grab that homewrecker by the hair. But I can't really blame her too much for it, she really did me a service. She brought me to my men.

"Don't!" That one word from my wolf has me standing straighter. *"Not yet."*

"I see you managed to get in with the Iron Beast Pack." She doesn't throw them a look, but the way she says their name in distaste, they definitely have history.

"Leave her alone," Az says with venom lacing every single word. I can't imagine what he's feeling.

Years of trying to track her, and she shows up at our doorstep. What they were trying to prevent is exactly what happened. I know this is going to be hard on him.

"Oh, Az." Her patronizing tone makes me want to slap her across the face.

"What are you doing here?" I ask her before she causes him to snap.

"Oh, I came here to collect." I don't like the sound of that. I look at the guys, baring their teeth aggressively.

She takes one step toward me and the knife flies, nearly stabbing her in the heart before she raises her hand to stop it. I gasp loudly and she chuckles like the lunatic she is. "What? Are you surprised?" She then throws the knife back too quickly for me to follow, even with shifter eyes. I only hear the loud groan from Az's lips. One look tells me she's stabbed him. He pulls it out of his shoulder, holding out the bloody knife with a cold smile. She doesn't seem fazed how he didn't cry out in pain.

"Before I was rudely interrupted by Aziel." His body stiffens and he glares at her with a promise of blood. "Dante, you can make your big appearance now." She rolls her eyes as if this whole thing is a fucking joke or a game that they're playing. Maybe it is for them but most definitely not for us.

As if we couldn't have any more surprises, the man in question shows up. Smirking at that. He waltzes in wearing an expensive Armani suit. What the hell would Theo think of this? You know what, never mind, I don't care.

His eyes zero in on me and then Ash. I think he knows what we did. I'm not going to look embarrassed though. I'm an adult, and I can be with whomever I want.

Az's nostrils flare as he looks at Dan like a cockroach he wants to step on.

"Why the hell won't this weasel die already," Ash growls venomously. I've never heard someone spit so much rage. I thought the way he spoke to me was bad, but this is another level.

"Didn't you know brother? Pussys have nine lives." Az smirks darkly, looking at Dan like he's about to rip him to pieces.

"How the hell did Dan think that this would end well? Az murdered countless members of Dan's pack, and that fool wants more?" Both my wolf and I narrow our eyes at our target. Make no mistake, that's what he is. He kidnapped my kids, he kidnapped me, and he tried to take me away, not once, but twice, and this will be the third time.

"He's going to wish he never met me," he says so silently it's like a vow to himself. No one but Tyler, Ash, and I can hear him.

Benji still looks empty standing on her side, and as much as I want to go to him, I stand still because I know she controls him.

"You just don't go the fuck away, do you?" Az asks, recovering just as quickly as the rest of the guys. He's so angry I'm surprised flames aren't coming out of his ears. He takes a protective stance in front of us. My eyes focus briefly at the exposed tattoos on his forearms before looking up at our threats.

"We kill them first and then we'll have sex. Blood bath and sex is a good combination," she chuckles darkly, and I still wonder how the hell we ended up together. But I really can't say that I disagree. I love her idea more than I want my human side to admit.

Their rage is all-consuming, and I can't imagine being cursed for this long.

"Yeah, who do you think helped Dante break through the barrier?" she laughs a high-pitched devilish laugh, one that I would associate with borderline lunacy. Hair prickles on my body.

Turning my attention to Dan I say, "So you thought that the woman my ex husband cheated on me with is the one that wants to save us both?" I wish I had my dagger with me. Now how the fuck am I going to defend everyone without it? If Krissy can't die any other way, how the hell am I going to kill her? At least with my weapon we have a chance, but I left it in my room. I didn't anticipate something like this happening.

Dan takes a step forward, but the men growl, and he thinks better of it. Good, either way this won't end well for him. He's fucked in my book. I don't care what happens to him anymore. I slightly wonder if Theo knows she's a witch and Dan's a shifter, you know what, not my fucking problem.

Oh shit, my kids! Where the fuck are they? Did Dan take them away again? My breathing picks up, and I see stars as I hyperventilate, nearly losing my shit. "They're fine, everyone is locked up in the school." Tyler answers my quiet panic, and I smile gratefully before turning my glare back at Dan.

"You really are a dumbass. First you turn Kat into a wolf, putting her in danger, then you kidnap her and her children and then try to kidnap her again in the woods, and to top it off, you were in an alliance with the woman her ex cheated on her with?" Az scoffs like he can't believe the ridiculousness of the situation. Truthfully, I'd be laughing hysterically too if this wasn't happening to me.

"Actually, you are pretty dumb, Dante." Krissy agrees. He looks at her with a frown on his face. "Do you really think I want to help you?" All I've ever wanted was to kill her, but it would have made Theo angry, and I really don't want to get on his bad side. I mean who would take care of the kids if Kat were gone?" The way she says my name with so much hate and venom you'd think I did her wrong somehow.

Dan sneers at her. I guess he really did think she was going to help him out. "Just remember you can't control me, the only ones you can control are the four of them and that's only because you were able to bind them. I'll get the council on you, Krissy. I'll tell them your location." His happy mood is suddenly gone.

"You can try, but they won't be able to catch me, and if they do, well then..." She looks at her fingernails like this is of no importance to her, like this is all just a waste of time having to deal with Dan. "I'll kill them." She shrugs nonchalantly.

Dan howls and shifts into a wolf, destroying the very expensive suit he was wearing. He runs after her and, with unnatural speed, she sidesteps him.

"Fuck, I can't move," Tyler growls.

"I can't either," Ash says. I look at them, raising an eyebrow. What's going on?

"Magic," Krissy says as she fights with Dan. Well, Dan is fighting trying to snap his teeth into her neck. I get a sense of déjà vu. Remembering when I was fighting for my life and thinking I was going to die and never see my kids again.

Only she sidesteps him. She's quicker and more calculated than he is. Is it because witches are much more skilled than wolves or is it because she has too much magic inside of her that gives her the boost to be able to do that?

"Oh, Dante. You're a fucking useless dog." She hits him in the face and he yelps, his wolf flying back and hitting a tree. I hear his back snap as he slides down. I try not to cringe, but that shit must have hurt.

He shakes it off, getting back up again. He's a little wobbly, but that doesn't stop him from getting back at her. Wow, he must have healed really fast if he's already up and running. My throat doesn't feel as scratchy but it's still healing as we speak. He growls and runs so fast that he's almost a blur. He bites her hard on her hand, and I hear the crunch of her bones breaking as she screams in pain.

"You little fucker! Good for nothing wolf." She charges at him with magic and he loosens his grip. "I will destroy you." She grabs a knife from her front pocket, and I gasp because this was me when Dan was trying to change me, and I grabbed a small knife trying to save myself. I try to look away, but I can't. My eyes are glued to the scene and my body won't move, not because she has a hold on me, but because my memory of this situation is too raw for me to handle.

Dan gets ready to jump, he wants to get behind her so he can attack her. She jumps and uses the knife when he is overhead. Everything happens in slow motion, but in reality, everything happens quickly. She cuts through his stomach and his intestines fall out. She quickly moves away and side steps all the blood. I finally look away, trying not to gag. He drops to the ground motionless. That wolf is definitely dead, there's no coming back from that.

Krissy pants, but not as hard as I think she should. "Grab her, Ash." He hesitates for a brief second before his eyes glaze over. He walks up behind me, grabbing my shoulders. "Az, show me the knife." He raises it up in the air with a vacant stare. "Now go stab Kat in the stomach." He walks up to me and I try to run."

"Az, please stop." I try to put in whatever magic I felt earlier, but it's not there. "Please stop, Az," I beg again as he comes closer to me, but his face is blank and he doesn't hear me.

When he's in front of me, I squeeze my eyes shut waiting for the pain. Ash lets go of my arms and I hear a grunt. I open my eyes in time to see Krissy and Amara facing each other. Az and Ash are on the floor a few feet away from me. Amara used her magic to blast them back. They shake their heads as if clearing their mind.

"Now, now big sister. I've just started my fun." Grabbing a hold of Amara's hair, she drags her along the ground and slams her down, keeping a heeled shoe on Amara's back. I should've known Amara's eyes looked familiar. I just couldn't pinpoint how similar they were. But as Amara's are gray and vibrant, Krissy's are dull and lifeless. She may possess all the power but it has drained her of her features. Don't get me wrong, as much as I want to think this woman is ugly, she's beautiful and perfect, but she looks detached from life.

"You four are under my control. I can make you do whatever the fuck I want." She smiles widely at each and every single one of us. We don't return it, but it doesn't seem to faze her. At least Benji's eyes no longer look glazed over like he's in a trance.

"So, Kitty Kat?" She imitates the nickname Benji calls me, and I can see the disgust in her face. She paces around in front of me, and I so wish I had my weapon to defend myself.

"I tapped your phone, well up until Tyler figured it out."

"Were you the one that attacked us at the bar?" I scrunch my brows.

She only smiles wickedly. "I should have known," Amara says from the ground.

"Did you ever figure out what the curse was?" I stay quiet but she continues anyway. "You see, some wolves have magic. There are just so few of them around now. These four men of yours have magic." She comes closer to me, leaving her sister behind on the ground. All I want to do is take a giant step back, but I keep my footing. I don't want to show her how much she's affecting me. "You know why this pack is called the Iron Beast." I already know this since Ash told me, but I make no movement. She gets closer to my ear and whispers, "Because they can control iron." She steps back, eyeing me, and I try to look surprised. "But of course, they don't have use of their magic because I took it." Az frowns heavily. He's ready to rip her head off if only he wasn't trapped by her magic. "They would have been the only ones that could stop me, and that's why as soon as I got all my powers, they were the first I binded."

Something here doesn't make sense. If the council wanted to kill me so badly because of my violet eyes, and I was a threat to their hierarchy, then Krissy here is a bigger threat. Even if I am or was powerful, wouldn't she be more dangerous because she knows how to wield her magic? "Why didn't the council do anything to you?" I mean surely they want to kill me, but don't they want to protect the rest of the supernaturals?

She gives me a high-pitched laugh. It's so sensitive to my ears. "Oh, dear Kat. They were the ones who hired me."

Chapter Thirty-four

Benji

Well fuck! The council, who's supposed to have the best interest of the supernaturals, hired Krissy to kill nearly all the witches in existence, but Kat, a newly turned wolf, was a threat. It doesn't make sense, but we should know better than anyone how deep their circles run.

I want to speak up and ask questions, but she has a tight hold on me. The magic leash she has on us is so secure I can barely move my fingers. The only one of us not tied down by her is Kat, and that's because she isn't bound.

"Hey Az, Ash, Tyler." Nothing but empty silence. She severed our connection long ago, but I wanted to try it to see if anything happened. Maybe if we were mated, we could have been able to communicate with each other, but as it stands, we're vulnerable to the witch.

Amara is instantly up in the air holding her throat. Krissy is using her magic to suffocate her and throws her against the tree. From the corner of my eye, Kat flinches, wanting to get to her, and I want to tell her not to move. Krissy is too dangerous and unpredictable. Since she got her magic, she's been unstable. She was nothing like this when I first met her. The power trip has obviously gotten to her.

From her position on the floor, Amara whimpers. "I don't understand, Krissy. Why did you do it?" Amara's voice breaks and my heart shatters for the amount of grief and sorrow showing in her eyes. She's on the floor drained of all her power.

We aren't in a good position right now.

Krissy shows no remorse. Nothing to show that she's upset about her sister's emotions. She's pure evil.

"For power," she laughs darkly. "Why else?" She makes it sound as though there is nothing else to life. "I was promised all the power and that we would rule together."

"By who?" She chokes on her words with dull, wet eyes. "That's still a secret," she says and winks at Kat. "No worries, I'll let you in on it right before I slit your throat." No, I can't let that happen. This is the first time we've all been happy in a long time. I can't let her destroy our light, our happiness. Even Ash and Az seem slightly different. I've finally found something worth fighting for, and I'm not just going to let that go.

"Oh... Oh but let me tell you," she says as she claps her hands and jumps up and down like a schoolgirl, and my stomach drops. She's too excited about this, which means nothing good will come of it.

"Do you want to know another secret?" she asks, toying with my Kitty Kat as if she hasn't suffered enough from this crazy bitch. As if she can't contain her excitement anymore, she continues. "When I wanted to get with the Iron Beast Pack and they turned me down, guess what I did?" Her eyes flicker with insanity. Not waiting for Kat to talk, she says, "I made Ash believe he found their mate." I think I stop breathing. I want to look at Ash to make sure he's okay. It's always been rough for him to talk about Emma, but hearing this... "I created a fake pull and connection. They both thought they were mates. Then I killed her right in front of him." The rage that consumes me is like no other. If I wasn't tied down, I would have slit her throat. Granted with all that power, she'd probably kill me first, but I can't think straight.

I can only imagine what Ash is feeling right now. He thought he wasn't able to protect our mate. He felt like such a failure for years and this is the biggest reason we let him lead. It gave him a sense of comfort when he believed that he could protect us. "I was so hurt, I wanted Ash and the pack to pay for it," she says with a fake pout on her lips. "You want to know something else, Kat? It was apparently written in the stars, two lunatic women spieled to the council when they thought the council could help." She waves her hand. "They said the Iron Beast Pack would find a powerful mate, but it would take years for them to find her, and when they mated, they'd be unstoppable." I swallow hard trying to push myself out of the invisible restraints. "They were supposed to be the next leaders for the shifters." She shrugs. "Oh well, I guess that won't be happening anymore, will it?" God, I just want to stab her and bleed her out. I'm not as bloodthirsty as Az but watching her bleed would be satisfying.

"And here the Iron Beast Pack thought they'd be avenging their lost mate, but in reality, she wasn't even theirs." She raises both her hands. "It was created by yours truly." She puts her hands down in satisfaction. She has us at a disadvantage and she knows it. She's thriving in this mess she's put us through.

"Anyway, they told the council they needed to find the woman with violet eyes and protect her. Well, the council doesn't like anyone that would be more powerful than them because it threatens their hierarchy," she says, folding her hands and touching her lip. "Although, there really is only one person that rules them," she says as an afterthought.

"Why are you telling me all this?" Kat's voice breaks. She hurts as much as we do. She cares for us deeply and she feels our pain. I want to hug and comfort her. I knew we were meant to be together. It felt right. My wolf, my body, everything belongs to her.

My mate.

"Because you guys won't survive," she says in a matter-of-fact way. Like anything we do will be useless, and I don't want to admit it, but it's not looking so great for us. "This is where it will all end," she says with a self-satisfied smirk, and I wish I could wipe it off her face. We can't let that happen. I'm not sure how we're going to stop her, but all I know is that we have to. "Too bad." She's walking away from Kat and up to me. "It seems like you all were actually destined to be with one another." My body is paralyzed, I can no longer move or breathe. I can feel the shift in the air as Ash roars. He was so certain Kat wasn't the one, even while he was drawn to her, he pushed her away every chance he got. Even going as far as blaming her for being turned.

Although Az wanted to hate her, he couldn't ignore the strange pull. He didn't want her, he was fighting it, even going as far as bringing two women home who had some resemblance to Kat, but it did nothing for him. He couldn't even go through with it. The only way he was satiated is when he finally had her. I'm sure Ash felt the same way earlier today, and I know he nearly mated with her. I can smell it all over them, he needs all of us to seal it and I'm planning on not dying tonight. I've only had her for almost a month. I need more time with her. This can't be it. I won't allow it.

"*Mate,*" my wolf growls in agreement, and I briefly wonder if he knew and that's why he was trying to get me to claim her.

Tyler believed the same way I did. We both knew we felt an instant connection. Tyler backed off in the beginning since she was still married, but then he thought better of it and went with his wolf instincts, and now, I know I can speak for all of us when I say we can't get enough of Kat.

If our spark was diminishing before, it has now been reignited knowing that Kat is our true mate. We will fight back.

Our girl looks determined too. She's already lost her best friend Jess. She has a glint in her eye, and I hope she doesn't try to do something crazy, but that's just wishful thinking.

Chapter Thirty-five

Kat

No one is looking at Amara but she's on the ground writing discreet symbols in the dirt. Krissy is looking at me while I hold onto the silver dagger behind my back. Moving my fingers through the ridges on the handle brings me comfort. No one saw it, but it came to me when I called it. It came to me when I desperately needed it for it to come. Sort of like Thor calling on his hammer. I call and it comes. This is how it will end for Krissy. This is how she dies, and I don't feel an ounce of guilt for wanting to kill her.

"Should that scare me, wolf?"

"No." That one word vibrates through my body, putting aside my human thoughts. At this moment,

I'm all animal. I don't care seeing the light leave her eyes. There is only one thing that I want and that is to be with my...mates.

It's strange but at the same time, it's not. My wolf knew all along. She tried to tell me to point things out. The way I hoard their clothes or want to be near their scent. She just didn't outright tell me because she knew I'd lose my mind and keep her in a tight cage. Sadly, I think she was right. I would have freaked out and left this place.

Now, having it confirmed brings me joy. I can understand the jealousy I felt toward any woman that came near them, it was because they were mine all along. My wolf told me that they were mine.

I'm playing with my weapon behind my back, putting on a scared face. I will drive it through her heart. I no longer fear this new life, my mates, my power. I'm tired of being afraid.

I don't know much about witches, but I think Amara is using her blood for something. For what? I have no clue yet. If the way her eyes drop in sadness is any indication, it has to do with killing her sister.

If I can prevent her from doing it, I'll take that burden away from her.

I'll have to bide my time and keep her talking. "What are you going to do with my kids?" I hope this will keep her chattering.

"Oh, those little shits..." Yeah, I'm zoning out now. Hearing her talk will only make me angrier, and I'll screw up. I only have one chance and I can't let her know I have the upper hand.

Az is next to me and there's a deep low growl coming from his throat. I look at the others, and they all have similar expressions. Good thing I'm not paying attention to her, what she's babbling about is obviously nothing good.

My whole focus is on Amara until Krissy looks at me again. Then I look back at her and she tilts her head expecting a reaction. Oh, that's right I'm supposed to be heartbroken. "Fuck you, Krissy," I spit out to satiate her hunger when she starts talking again. I want to roll my eyes, but don't dare make such a gesture.

She laughs again in contentment when the ground begins to shake violently. I'm brought to my knees and so are the others. "What are you doing, Krissy?" Ash questions.

"It's not me," she chokes out, looking at each of us in turn, trying to figure out who is causing the earth to quake beneath our feet. I look away from Amara and put on a frightened face, which I suppose isn't hard to do because I'm sort of freaking out right now. Hundreds of spirits surround us, and my whole body shivers at the sight of so many towering wisps of dead people. I feel just as trapped as my guys, but no magical ropes are binding me in place. As soon as I get the opportunity, I'm going to stab that witch to death.

Finally, Krissy turns slowly, coming around to face Amara. "No…no…" she stutters, backing away, and for the first time, she looks horrified. I would be celebrating if I wasn't panicking too. Even my men have their eyes wide open. "I killed you all," she stammers, looking around at the gathering spirits, and it dawns on me, these are the witches she killed, her ancestors.

This is my chance to stab her while she's distracted, but before I can act, very familiar arrows slam down on her, hitting her shoulders. She screeches loudly but doesn't go down. "No," she gasps again as if that's the only word she knows how to say amongst this chaos.

From the corner of my eyes, the men start to twitch. I don't dare watch them from fear that Krissy will notice. "You promised me her powers. I'm going to kill Kat." My body shivers. I guess her brain started working again. Does this lady really hate me that much? I seriously don't know what the fuck I did to deserve this. "I know Kat has the magic. It's just hidden somewhere." She looks at me with so much hate in those deep, dull gray eyes of hers.

I look around feeling baffled, trying to figure who she's talking to. Is some other person or spirit here that I can't see?

"She probably has direct contact with someone," Benji says, and I nod my head slowly up and down in understanding. I guess that makes sense, right?

"The same way we will communicate when we bond." Umm...what? "We'll have a connection with each other, but hers is made with the power she's gained." Well fuck! I don't know if I want the guys hearing my thoughts twenty-four seven.

"Task at hand Kat. We can focus on this later. But if we don't manage to kill the witch, she'll surely kill us all." She's right, we won't have another chance like this one. The only reason we have a chance is because she loves hearing herself talk.

"You will come with us now." A lady with gray eyes and red hair comes up to her, she looks like a cross between Amara and Krissy. When another arrow crosses through her body aiming directly at Krissy. Who the fuck is shooting at her? The arrows aren't doing shit. But these are the same one's the hunters used.

She screams and uses her powers to blast them. The translucent figures don't go too far. Those arrows might not bring her down completely, but her magic is becoming dull. Probably the reason the guys are able to move but only slightly.

She starts chanting something foreign to my ears. "Kat, kill her before she completes the spell," Amara croaks out. I hurry to try to get to her when the ground begins to shake again, throwing me off my trail. Amara and I both get thrown around on the ground.

A loud burst of power comes through the ground and there's black smoke. I can't see what's in front of me. I start to panic. My head goes to the worst-case scenarios, and I think I end up in another universe. I blame my overactive imagination on all of the supernatural movies I've watched.

I lift my hand, but even with my wolf vision, I can't see anything else. My body trembles from the cold, and I haven't gotten cold once since I turned to a shifter.

I'm going to open my mouth to scream and yell for help when I hear her. "I'm not going to die you asshole." Clearly, she's talking to someone who isn't here. Her body convulses as blood runs down her mouth.

The blackness begins to clear and she looks at me again. "He will take you and your men won't be able to protect you." She sounds self-satisfied, and I honestly don't know what I did to this woman for her to hate me so much. She's the one that took my husband away from me. I briefly wonder if he's going to mourn her death when I kill her tonight, and I feel a pang of jealousy that he'd care about this woman more than me. But then I look around, realizing I don't need him to care, not anymore. I don't need Theo or his approval.

"What have you done?" her sister asks, her voice weak with terror. Krissy turns to look at Amara and I run up to her. This is my chance. She's too distracted to notice. I swiftly run, hiding my weapon behind my back, and at the last minute, she sees me coming. She's trying to ward off the spirits she killed to gain her power, but they're furious and not backing down. If I were her, I'd be running for the hills. Since I know they're not here for me, I'm not panicking too hard. I'm still scared of course, but not like I was earlier.

I run to her right, but she hits me on the side of the face with the palm of her hand and I go down. There's a low growl behind me, and I know my men are trying to get out of their hold and tear her to pieces. I can taste their violence in the air. They wanted her to die all those years ago, but now that she's laid a hand on me, they won't forget.

I grab her hair and pull her back, trying to take a chunk of her neck, but she headbutts me. Moisture gushes from my nose and I know she's broken it. Fuck that hurts!

The blinding pain sends a wave of heat through my body as I scurry along the ground and grab for my weapon. There's a sharp pain in my ankles as hands like a vice pull me back. I sink my nails into the soft grass beneath me, clawing and reaching with fierce determination, but Krissy is too strong to fight this way. When I look up, there's a flare of panic and recognition in her eyes as she sees the Kiss of Death for the first time. She's terrified, and

I can't help the slow smile that spreads across my face.

She lands on top of me, and I can feel the metal ridges of my weapon. My hand is laid open and she has an iron grip on my wrist preventing my hand from constricting. I briefly look to my side where my guys are, and they're struggling to get out of her hold, but there's more movement now. As much as they want to help me, they can't, they're still stuck.

It's all on me. I have to kill her.

I hit her nose with my forehead the way she did with me, and blood gushes from her nostrils. "Ah, you bitch," she screams. I wish I could bask in that glory but there's no time. I have to end this. I have to end her. As long as she lives, she puts my pack—my family—in danger.

While she's nursing her nose, I get the opportunity to get on top of her and grab her by the neck. My talons come out in mid-shift. My mouth turns into a muzzle.

I squeeze her neck hard until crimson trails run down my arm. I have the urge to lick the blood off my hands, but my human side quickly kicks in, telling me to hold off on that gory thought.

She's harder to kill, not only because she's a witch and has magic, but also because she's supernatural. If she were a human, I'd be able to rip her neck with one long squeeze, but she's not, so her neck is hard as bricks. This lets me know that I'll have to thrust the dagger harder and deeper if I want to truly end her life. In the back of my head, my human side cowers at my violent thoughts, but I ignore that bit. If she comes out again, I'll lose the leverage I've worked so hard to gain.

With one arm on her neck, I try to feel around for my trusty weapon but remember I can call it now. I can't believe I once thought it was useless metal. I call to it, and it comes to me. Krissy's eyes widen and I sit there for a long moment, watching her pupils dilate. I bask in her terror. I know that's fucked up, but my wolf is savage.

She fights me by grabbing my long strands, but my sole focus is driving the purple blade through her heart and ending her life once and for all. She pushes my hand away, and I remember the time where I was trying to hold off the wolf, which I didn't know was Dan, but she fights the way I did. I feel powerful in this second, and I wonder if he felt the same as he was trying to bite my neck. I'm inching closer, her arms getting weaker.

Her gaze shifts to one of horror. She knows it is a great possibility that her life will end tonight. The tip of the weapon points to her heart, and just that small contact sears her flesh. There is a quick burst of power coming from her and the Kiss of Death goes up. I tentatively look up to watch my men surrounding us. She had to take off the hold she had on them to use her power to try and get the weapon from me. My men grab my hands, pushing the tip of the purple steel down again. Even though she's weakened, she's still strong. My hand wobbles, but the guys are helping me keep it steady. It finally sinks through her flesh, and the sound the metal makes when meeting bone doesn't scare me. I may be more ruthless since turning into a shifter, but I won't let anyone take control of me ever again.

She points to me one last time, her body convulsing. "I was right," she gurgles, the blood seeping from her mouth. "It was in the tattoo all along." She takes her last ragged breath, and the tension leaves her body.

Confused, I hesitantly bring my bloodied hand up to touch my heart tattoo that's been there for sixteen years. "There's nothing there," Tyler says, reaching over Krissy's body and pulling my hand from my cheek. I got this tattoo so long ago, even before I married Theo.

Jess and I... Jess, how I miss my friend. My super secretive friend. Could she have done something to me when we got tattoos all those years ago? Altered me somehow?

Before I break down in a sob, I push the thoughts away and focus on what's in front of me.

We all stand up, watching the smoke that levitates from Krissy's body with wide eyes as the essence she stole leaves her. "What the hell is that?" Benji is the bravest out of all of us for speaking up first. I was too afraid to talk, not wanting to get the attention of whatever that thing is flowing in the air.

"That is all the magic from my ancestors," Amara says with watery eyes. With all that blood on her face it would be hard to miss, but not to us, not to wolves. Our eyesight is better than most. The tears roll down her face. "They're looking for another host." I drag my eyes back to the pink and purple plume of smoke, what I now know is magic.

"Why isn't it dying with Krissy?" Ash asks with an eyebrow raised in genuine confusion.

"It looks like the magic wants to be let free." With that, her ancestors start disappearing one by one, but there's one that lingers for a while. Amara excuses herself. "Mom," she cries, and I turn away to give her privacy.

"What does this mean?" Az asks. I didn't notice before because I was so focused by the winding of colors, but he has his bloodied tattooed hand on my lower stomach, not quite touching me, but it's there to protect me against any dangers. My heart flutters at his nice gesture. I wonder if he even knows he's doing it.

The colors hover for another moment until they finally fly away. "So, someone is going to be getting all that magic? For what purpose?"

"I'm only guessing here, but it looks like dark times are ahead." Seriously more dark times. I've turned into a wolf for almost a month and my whole life goes in a completely different direction from what I would consider normal. I look to my right, seeing Az walk up next to Tyler watching the light fly away, and then I look to my left, watching Ash and Benji stare out into the distance. As I observe my men, I realize that I wouldn't have it any other way. Mates? That's what these men are. A part of my world. Something I can't turn my back on. I'd go through the most dangerous challenges just so we could be together.

Even Ash and Az, the two most stubborn men I've ever met, I'd do anything for them. I touch my face, my hands coming away with tears. I look down at my wet fingers, and when I look up, I'm surrounded by all of them.

The emotions going through Ash are so raw. He thought he had a mate and he lost her. He was pushing me away because he thought it was a betrayal to the woman he failed. I admire his dedication.

"Katarina," Ash faces me, "I—"

"It's okay Ash, you don't have to say anything." I look down at the ground before looking back up.

"I'm so sorry." He says softly.

I walk a step closer to him, but he's on me before I can take another one. We're a bloodied mess but it doesn't matter. He claims my mouth and I give in. He's apologizing to me for being so cruel, for not sticking up for me, and in turn, I show him that I understand, and I know his loyalty runs deep because that's what it truly was. He messed around with women after he lost Emma, but with me there was a connection, and I can't blame him.

His mouth is demanding more and I give it to him. It's a dance that we're playing, pushing and pulling. He's all I need to be able to breathe. I'm so consumed by our joint kiss I nearly forget we have an audience. It doesn't matter though; we have a lifetime to explore each other.

We pull apart, both of us panting. There's so much grief in his eyes, and I wish that I could make it better for him, but it's something he'll have to process himself. I'll be nearby in case he needs me. I'll always be around.

Both Krissy and Dan are dead. I wonder how Theo will feel knowing that his close friends are no longer alive.

On the outside, it may look like an act of revenge, me going on a killing spree, but the truth is, that's not how it went down. It's crazy to think that it could have gone a completely different direction.

I decided to let go of that anger, let go of the person I became when I married him. Now everything he holds dearly is gone. I almost feel sorry for him, but I don't. Maybe that makes me a bad person, but I can't bring myself to care. He's brought me a lot of pain over the years, and it wasn't until I was free from him did I realize how much baggage I was carrying.

It's hard to believe that all our problems were rooted in Krissy, but now that she's gone for good, we have a lot of living to catch up on. Though, something doesn't seem quite right. I want to brush the uneasy feeling off as an adrenaline crash, but there's a dark feeling coming over me, and I fear that Krissy was only the surface of what's to come.

Chapter Thirty-six

Tyler

My phone rings, startling all of us. I grab it from my pocket and turn it over. "Tyler, something is wrong!" There's panic on the other side of the call. I hold tightly to my phone watching my brothers, and Kat's violet eyes are on me.

"What's going on, Ryder?" I try to stay calm. Benji slightly stiffens, Az's hands clench into fists, Ash is wearing a scowl, and they all look like they're ready to lose their shit. One of us has to remain calm.

"Are you where I left you?" For some reason, I already know the answer to my own question.

"No." Motherfucking kids.

"Where the hell are you then?" My calming temper vanishes as soon as Ava's scream comes through the phone.

Kat snatches the phone. "Where are you guys?" Her voice is breathy and I'm afraid she's going to have a panic attack when another pained wail comes through the phone.

"At the cabin." She looks at me, and I can see the question in her eyes. She wants to know if I can take her to them. I nod my head in confirmation, and that seems to relax her a bit, but only slightly.

"How far is it?" Kat asks me while Benji wraps his arms around her waist letting her know she's not alone. He kisses her neck gently but purely out of the need to comfort her. He wants her to know that he's there.

"You guys need to hurry," Zay growls as Kat flips the call to speaker. He's trying to fight someone, and I think that someone is Ava. I don't dare tell Kat unless I'm positive that's what it is. I look at the other guys and their silence mirrors my own. No reason to freak Kat out further.

"I'll go get the truck," Ash says. We're all a bloodied mess but there's no time for showers. We all need to figure out what the hell is going on.

A minute later, he pulls the truck in front of us and we get in. Kat, Benji, and I are in the back. Az climbs into the passenger seat, and as soon as the doors close, we haul ass.

I take the phone from Kat since she doesn't look like she can talk. Benji pulls her onto his lap as she stares blankly out the window. I wish I was the one comforting her right now. She looks like she needs it.

"What's going on now?" I don't dare hang up until we're there.

"She's whimpering." I look over at Kat and she keeps her eyes tightly shut. "I want to hold her," Zay says softly, almost to himself.

"Don't touch her. Not until we get there," I warn.

"Fuck it," Cash says so softly I almost didn't hear it.

"No. Cash, don't even think about it." And because he's the quiet one that does whatever the fuck he wants I add, "That's an Alpha's order." I hear him grumble, probably cussing me out right now. I don't want anyone touching her until we have an idea of what's going on.

Az is talking on the phone, and I hear Amara's voice on the other side of the call. By the sounds of it, Amara is on her way and bringing Doc with her. Probably a good idea and good thinking on Az's part.

I just hope Amara is going to be okay to deal with whatever this is. It's been an emotional day, especially for her, and she really needs to rest up and take a vacation, but instead, we're dragging her further into the woods because something is wrong.

She's been through so much over the years with her sister, she deserves some time. After this, I'm talking the guys into giving her some space.

There's another loud yelp, and I look over at Kat's stiffening body as she curls into Benji. Her face is on his chest and she's grabbing his shirt tightly.

I wasn't thinking before with everything going on. "What did you guys do?" I try not to sound accusing but that's the way it comes out. "Is she hurt?"

"We didn't fucking do anything," Zay growls. Something about all this doesn't sound right. I'm trying not to speculate or put any blame on anyone, but something doesn't sit right.

Ash is driving like a maniac over dirt roads and open fields trying to get there quickly, and no one seems to care about the jarring ride. With one of the big bumps in the field, my phone falls from my hand and between the seats. The kid's voice is muffled, but we're almost there.

"Fuck, I'm scared," Kat tells us. "I knew she wasn't well but believed it was all the changes we've been through."

I want to tell her everything will be fine, but I don't know if it will be for sure. So we all keep quiet, anxiety running through the roof waiting for what we're going to find there.

When we get to the cabin, we all open the door before Ash puts it in park. Az bursts through the front door of the cabin and we all storm in behind him, following the noise to one of the master bedrooms. This is a vacation spot for our wolves. It's sitting on a lake and the best part is no humans can get here. It's secluded from everything.

Ava is on the bed with Cash, Ryker, Zayden, and Bryson surrounding her. We come closer and they collectively growl at us.

Kat looks startled, but they aren't growling at her, and she knows they aren't either, but it doesn't stop her from being surprised. She gets closer to the bed, and although the guys don't growl at her, they stiffen, watching her every move.

"What happened?" Ash's voice fills the air in the room. His eyes are alert looking for a threat.

"We don't know," Bryson says as he keeps his eyes on a moaning Ava.

"Mija, I'm here," Kat calls out to her daughter in a soothing voice. She opens her eyes and there's a collective gasp around the room.

"What the fuck!" Kat pushes her daughter's hair from her forehead. "Shit, shit, shit. This is not good."

She spoke too soon, and her daughter's body starts to readjust. "What in the hell is going on?" one of them says, but my mind is completely confused. My eyes are on Kat as she starts sobbing next to her daughter.

"Alpha, we need to take care of her." Cash is the only soft spoken of the four of them. He's the one who is silent but deadly. Just like Az, but unlike Az, he hasn't learned how to deal with his trauma. He could potentially be dangerous. "If this is what we think it is...we need to stay."

"What does he mean?" Kat looks baffled, and I don't know how to answer the next part.

"Katarina," Ash says slowly as if he's speaking gently to a child. "Your daughter is shifting."

"Shifting into what?"

Benji comes closer to her, bends down, and nuzzles her neck to calm her down before speaking.

"A wolf."

Chapter Thirty-seven

???

"Sir we've come with news." My three advisers come in. My back is turned to them.

I'm looking at the big city. It's still early enough that there aren't many cars on the road, just the way I like it. I have a huge window with a clear view of the water. There's a couple walking on the sidewalk holding their Starbucks coffee mugs, tugging their coat a little tighter for warmth.

There was a time long ago when not very many cars roamed the streets. It was simpler back then. With no phones and no cameras for people to invade your privacy. Now my kind has to fear humans finding out about us and trying to kill us.

That's what those worthless humans do, they try to kill anything that's unknown to them.

It used to only be hunters, but I got them on my side. Got them to fight for us and do our bidding.

I grab the glass of scotch from my desk, already preparing myself for the bad news, but then I think better of it and grab the water instead. I don't want to get drunk this early in the morning. Especially when I know I have to put plans in motion. "Go on," I tell him harshly. The mousy man dressed in the same expensive type of suit that I'm wearing looks widely around the room, afraid that something will pop up from the shadows.

The corner of my mouth twitches slightly, pouring the cool water down my throat. I love smelling their fear.

"The witch has died, and the Iron Beast Pack curse has been lifted." I tighten my grip on my glass cup and it breaks, soaking my freshly pressed slacks. My jaw clenches. Those four are a pain in my ass. Once they knew I could no longer control them, they left. We acted like it was our wish, but the reality is that they were too powerful to stop.

"There's another thing sir." He doesn't reek of fear as much as the other two, but he's still scared. Good, they all should be.

"Well spit it out," I tell them when no one speaks up.

"We think the kids have power as well...or at least the girl does." My body tenses. Shit, and they no longer have trackers on their phones.

I don't show any reaction of course, but my interest is piqued. "How did you come up with that conclusion?" I ask nonchalantly, but my whole body is tense.

"One of the hunters told us. He got close to them but not close enough that they'd be detected." I nod my head. My plans have changed. I almost allow myself a small smile when the last one voices. "The witch said it's in the heart tattoo before she died. So, Kat does have the power." If Kat has it in her and it's merely been suppressed, then he's right. That's how Jess did it.

It would make sense. Jess wouldn't tell me, so I killed her. Kat is too powerful to be paired up with those mutts, they'll be a force to be reckoned with. I can't let that happen. My family has led this community for generations. There is no way in hell we're giving up that power.

Then that means... "Is that all?" I say, sounding aggravated. He nods his head and they quickly leave the room.

"She let it free." Finally, one good thing that bitch did. She had me waiting for a long time. I had to play nice with her. I made a pact with her that if she was close to dying, she needed to release the shadows. Even against her will. She didn't want to, of course.

It would drain her of nearly all her magic, and she was too cocky with it.

I sit on my chair, grab my cell phone from my pocket, and begin dialing her number, she picks up on the third ring "Kat, I want shared custody of our kids."

Other books by Angelica

Iron Beast Pack Series
Marked Wolf

https://amzn.to/3jYhRH5

Chosen Wolf
Pre-Order

The Forgotten Series

The Forgotten World of the Witches

https://amzn.to/3Psza1y

The Forgotten world of the Jaguar Warriors

https://books2read.com/u/4DxRk7

The Forgotten World of the Faeries (Coming Soon)

Follow Me

Newsletter:

https://www.subscribepage.com/h1r6g8

FB Group:

https://www.facebook.com/groups/1107819209697-422

Instagram:

https://www.instagram.com/angelicaaquilesauthor-/

TikTok:

http://tiktok.com/@angelicaaquilesauthor

Acknowledgements

Thank you to my beta team Brenda, Faith, Karlie, Michelle, Nattiee, and Oriane for reading my book and giving me all the suggestions. I appreciate you ladies so much.

Thank you Heather for helping me out. You're a badass working with a newborn and taking on my book! I admire you so much!

Thank you Ari. You've helped me so much. I've been a mess because of my move and you have really helped me out! I really appreciate your time and I'm grateful to have you in my author journey.

Thank you Hope Brown for creating beautiful graphics and games.

Thank you to my husband and my kids. I wouldn't have been able to follow through without them. My husband for believing in me and knowing that this is the path that I'm meant to be on. For reminding me that this is exactly what I want to do even when I get sidetracked and try to work on other stuff. My kids for watching put hours and hours into writing and being so patient, well, as patient as they could be. I love you guys so much! I hope you see that mommy is following her dreams and I hope it gives you the motivation to follow your own.

Last but not least to my readers. Thank you so much for following Kat's journey. I really wanted to have a book where it wasn't a younger woman but a badass mom. I can't thank you enough for picking this book and reading it. I can't wait to bring you the next book in the series. Thank you all for giving this book a chance from the bottom of my heart thank you! I can't wait to bring you guys the next book.

About Me

Angelica Aquiles currently lives in California with her two sons, her husband, and her dog. She goes out fishing, hiking, and offroading with her family. When she has downtime she loves to get lost in a good book.

Made in the USA
Coppell, TX
19 June 2022